ST VALENTINE'S SECRET AGENT

Barbara Morgan

ISBN 978-1-915077-96-7

Website: http://www.ghostlywhisper.com

Facebook: https://www.facebook.com/ghostlywhisperltd

Instagram: https://www.instagram.com/ghostlywhisperltd

Twitter: https://twitter.com/GW_BooksEtc

Whisper of the Heart

CHAPTER 1

Julie

It's still quite far; I realize that. So, I shouldn't already feel this sense of oppression gripping my throat, threatening to choke me.

While leafing through the last cookbook I bought in Eason on O'Connell Street, in an unmissable special offer, I quickly check my diary that I almost always have to hand. Yes, it's only January 25th. And what should upset me most now is this cold that creeps into my bones, this icy wind that seems to pierce my skin like a thousand tiny pins of ice were all pointed at me in battle gear.

I admit it also because it would be useless to deny it. I'm allergic to Valentine's Day. I start thinking about it in mid-January when, with Christmas left behind by now, we begin to breathe the now very distinguishable (at least for me) and infamous air of the feast of love, with chocolate hearts and shop windows decorated for the occasion. As for me, if I have absolute certainty in life, it's that on February 14th, I inevitably spend it alone. Even if I had a boyfriend madly in love with me until the day before, it has always been like that. I have the proof.

Likely, Valentine's Day is probably allergic to me. This awareness has made that day even more depressing for me than Christmas is for some. But I know there is no Grinch for the Day of Love. We should invent one.

Could it be worse for me? Maybe not. Apart from the fact that my name is Julie. Juliette, actually. In short, it is the most romantic and unfortunate female character in the history of world literature. I call myself Julie, anyway. Better not to rage.

Dublin's weather doesn't help. They also say that this year's winter is likely to be freezing, with a cold that hasn't been so bitter for a long time. Can it get any worse than now? I don't even want to know.

Returning to the feast of resigned solitude, at least for me, the problem is not me. Because I have been resigned for several years, I stopped counting them for a while. The problem is with my friend Valerie.

Yes, my best friend, Valerie, who should have married her boyfriend, Trent "The asshole" Richards, on Valentine's Day.

"Should have" are, in this circumstance, the keywords. In every situation, someone says that one should find comfort in the fact that it could have been worse. Some have been dumped directly at the altar, I admit it.

No, no... not me! At least I avoided that for the moment.

So, to recap... I'm planning an effective way to mitigate Valerie's suffering and discomfort. When these things happen, pain is often accompanied by the inescapable need to explain to the rest of the world that, unfortunately, nothing is going to happen anymore. All over, end of the story. Thank you for participating (metaphorically); go back home and enjoy this succulent and delicious gossip news. Because I increasingly realize that the world, or at least part of it, feels an almost devious pleasure in enjoying the misfortunes of others.

Maybe I'm exaggerating. However, I had to take charge of cancelling everything for Valerie and giving explanations to friends and relatives. It was one of the saddest and most embarrassing tasks of my life. My friend Valerie Renaud comes from a large family where everyone is close. So, she has a certain number of relatives and, if not really friends, an immense number of acquaintances of her parents. If it ever happens to me, at least from this point of view, I would be luckier.

I'm also reflecting on what I would like someone to do for me if I find myself in the same circumstance. I sigh, lowering my look to my new cookbook, full of colourful and inviting images. Maybe not a potato pie or a stuffed turkey...

No, it would take something more stimulating. I leave the book, beautiful but heavy like a boulder, and move from the small armchair to the chair next to the table where I left my laptop.

I start looking. I don't even know what, really. A kind of party? Or maybe a male striptease is better? Okay, no. Too depressing! But what then...? No, I didn't think they offered such things... full service! I will look in the meantime. Nothing will come of it, but I look at it. Except that some shows risk bringing even more sadness rather than fun. Like a hangover. So much joy and ease at the beginning, then sadness, melancholy, loneliness, and nausea. No, it's not good, not even as a joke. I would just risk emphasising the issue.

Probably the only thing Valerie wants is for Trent to think it over and return to her. That is precisely what she kept repeating until two weeks ago. The only thing worse than being dumped before Valentine's Day, the date set for your wedding, is to be dumped just after Christmas. Valerie got both.

I don't think he will reconsider, Trent. Not for nothing is known as Trent "The asshole" Richards. Usually, I never call him that in front of Val (okay, sometimes I miss it!) so as not to emphasise the issue. But he is an asshole. I thought this even before. He has an asshole attitude. That could have also been a sexy asshole, irresistible asshole. But no way. Trent is a nasty asshole, know-it-all asshole. He was also like that in France, where he and Valerie met. But she fell in love with him. And besides, I made the same mistake repeatedly with other specimens of... yes, I really have to say it... of an asshole.

I'm inclined to use swear words, especially when I'm nervous. And when I start thinking in a language that is not mine, they seem less and less hurtful and offensive to me.

Anyway, back to Val. Maybe I could find her another boyfriend. As they say... on the rebound, just to fill the void. Yes, a new boyfriend. As if he fell out of the sky.

I give up any other absurd search and pass to my faithful companion, my life's last and only love. Netflix. I need to catch up with the series of Christmas romantic comedies I had added to my list. I should make up. Or I could try going out, catching some more cold, throwing myself into a random pub and getting to know someone. It works like this here, at least, they say. I have yet to try it. But one of these days... yes, one of these days, I will do it. Maybe the man of dreams (I don't know if mine, Valerie's, or another woman's) is hiding right behind or in front of a pub counter and, at this very moment, is sipping a Guinness.

Giles

I knew it. Of course, I knew it. It was clear that sooner or later, I would be in trouble! But getting fired by my boss for finding me with the zipper of my trousers unfastened in front of his wife was too much! And then... had I unfastened it, at least! It had awkwardly caught on Annette Trask's bracelet, and... Gerrit drew the appropriate conclusions.

All right, I admit it. We were already fumbling in that area, but in the specific circumstance in which Gerrit Trask appeared, it wasn't wanted at all, at least on my part. But as the gentleman I am (or at least I should try to be), I took most of the blame. The outcome wouldn't have changed anyway.

Annette was in (fake) tears, Gerrit Trask was pissed like a bison on the attack and I... hell out of there! He really looked like a bison; I swear I saw the smoke coming out of his nostrils!

The most embarrassing thing is that we could not "release" Annette's bracelet, so it stayed there, like a souvenir attached to my... But it could have been worse for me. If the bracelet had been valuable and the Trasks had demanded it, I could have ended up in Henry Street, close to Jervis Shopping Centre, down to my smalls. Not only in a figurative sense.

Had I done something, at least, over the past few months. I avoid telling Michael because, knowing him, I know he would take the piss out of me for the rest of my life. And he would roar with laughter, calling me a chronic clumsy idiot. Because he, Michael, would have really got off with Annette. And I'm pretty sure he would have done it even under Gerrit's nose, being very cleverly able not to be caught by the boss.

My poor and embarrassing result is that having been out of work, I soon risk being left without money. Or I'll never, and I stress never, be able to pay the rent for the apartment on Parnell Street that I share with my cousin Michael Wrighton.

Actually, we are second or third cousins; I have not investigated. He moved to England with his mother when he was only a few years old, even though he was born in America. Then he arrived in Ireland, where we met about six months ago when I moved from New Jersey. Our grandparents were cousins, that's it.

It's almost certain that the bison Gerrit Trask won't take me back, even if he risks going bankrupt without me. I understood his character in the limited three months I worked with him. I say "almost certain" because I would bet my life on nothing and nobody now.

On the contrary, I cannot (and above all, I don't want to) go back to America. Not in New York, where I lived the last ten years since I started attending Columbia University and then abandoned it halfway.

My grandfather Séamus encouraged me to choose Ireland as a destination, even though I would have preferred Spain or

9

Portugal because, besides the continent, I would have gladly changed the climate as well. And I felt the moral obligation to please him as if it was the last wish of a convict. To be clear... I too often feel the moral obligation to please everyone. This also resulted in a mess with the Trasks.

But back to my sprightly grandpa, who is healthier than I am right now. He sent me here, he said, to look for our roots. I have never understood this matter of the roots. Who cares about the roots? If his parents wanted to eradicate themselves, they would have had their reasons. Serious reasons, I know that. It was a tough time, and staying in Ireland would have been a challenge. Like moving to the other side of the world and starting all over again. Which is the same thing I did almost a century later. Returning to the starting point, though.

The truth is I wouldn't even know where to start looking for these roots. I've found Michael, though. My grandfather and his had been speaking on the phone for many years. Michael's grandfather had lived in the United States, only to go back. His daughter Elize, Michael's mother, had married a guy from Phoenix, then moved to live in London with her two children, Michael and his sister Jennifer.

In short, as often happens lately, I contacted Michael on Facebook after some research. I remember seeing him only a few times during childhood, and he wasn't very friendly. He gave me a shove, threw me to the ground and made my nose bleed.

I arrived in Dublin, where Michael has lived for several years; I am trying to remember how many, choosing the capital instead of the surroundings of Cork, where our family comes from. I will go there sooner or later. Or maybe not. When I told Michael about my grandfather's request, he reacted with a shrug. We still have relatives there, that's for sure. But in all these years, he has never felt the need to go and look for them. He says your roots are where your ass is right now. It's not very Irish as an idea. Not even American. But I don't think I can blame him. Maybe I wouldn't have expressed it that way, but I think the same way, after all. I pretend to stay here looking for roots that, for me, have never had particular significance or importance. I left behind a life and a story that was no longer mine. The end of a chapter, the beginning of another. But probably, this new chapter won't last very long. It may already have ended or finished within a few days, anyway.

CHAPTER 2

Julie

It took me a while to get used to life here. I'm still working on it, as it's fashionable to say.

Valerie and I live in the Rathmines area, which is alright but rather expensive. It is central and well-connected, at least. We have been lucky because we found a reasonably affordable apartment to rent. It is very small but comfortable for us, even if, at times, the sense of oppression I feel inside pushes me to face the cold outside.

I've been here for about eight months, and after living a few years in Paris, I needed a change. In Geneva, where I was born, I didn't have much left to return to after the umpteenth and more recent heartbreak. But the truth is that I felt the absolute need to find a place without ties. So, I took advantage of Valerie's move to try to follow her. Initially, to help her settle in, despite having Trent, "The asshole", to protect her. Once again, I didn't realize that certain relationships don't protect but destroy.

Nobody really protects us. We are alone; this is the truth. We are alone. Like me on Valentine's Day. I no longer believe in love. How could I?

If there weren't some tragedy, my situation would be almost comical. I possess a fantastic ability; it's innate, but I could have refined it over the years to be dumped and remain hopelessly single on Valentine's Day. I was dumped the day before. I was also left atop the Eiffel Tower when I thought my boyfriend would do something else. From how he checked his jacket pockets and the languid look he gave me, I was almost convinced that he was about to get on his knees (or maybe not, let's not go that far), but anyway... Then I found out, to my extreme disappointment, that he was looking for his cell phone and that his new girlfriend (the one he replaced me with shortly after) wanted to know if he had already "finished" with me. Now I talk about it quietly, but... but in fact, maybe it's better not to talk about it at all. It was, however, very early for such a proposal. We had only been dating for two weeks. Better that way, as I wouldn't have known how to get myself off the hook.

The truth... yes, in short, the truth is that I'm still hurting from it. It would sting anyone, wouldn't it? It stung me even more when I was left while he was driving to a party. From Geneva, we had left and found ourselves in the middle of the French countryside, over the Swiss border. So, I couldn't even ask him to let me get out and disappear. I had to put up with the party and wait for someone else to take me home.

The worst thing was that Elton John's tune *Something about the way you look tonight* came in the background from the car radio of that bastard car. Here, the song's words clashed so horribly with the words of that cynical monster, my ex, that I... that I partly followed Elton, partly I followed him. And finally, I laughed in his face because it all seemed like a joke. But I realized immediately that he couldn't have planned it on purpose. The idiot didn't even know English enough to plan something so sneaky. And the song didn't come from one of his CDs, so it all happened in a purely and sadistically random way.

This is one of the reasons why, after a brief stop in Paris, I didn't return to Geneva. And I could no longer listen to *Something about the way you look tonight* in the same way. That is with a romantic and dreamy spirit, as would be appropriate for the song's lyrics and music. I mean, he ruined it for me! As I hear it, even by chance, I see myself in front of him, his idiotic expression, his car in the middle of nowhere... Yes, he, who was certainly not paying attention to the song's words, that I, instead, had started to follow more carefully than usual, distracting me from his words. He was only concerned about leaving me as quickly as possible to officially get together with someone else waiting for him at that party.

However, this situation has undauntedly repeated itself since high school. So, I'm starting to believe it doesn't depend on the asshole in question but on me. It almost seems like a curse. My first boyfriend left me with a note on February 12th.

So... on the Eiffel Tower, by letter, in music... now I only expect the plane with the sign and the fireworks with the words "Goodbye Julie Bonnet, I leave you, get yourself a new life." I got over it, but the idea that my stories fail around that date is almost scary. I left someone too, okay... but at other times, at least.

This also means that I have never been able to undertake lasting relationships despite having tried to commit myself to believing it. And this is rather sad and demeaning. But I try not to think about it now; I prefer to concentrate on Valerie, who is much worse off now than me.

At Christmas and New Year, at least, there is a sort of consolation of human solidarity in being single. Not on Valentine's Day. Especially if you are single against your will, like me and Valerie. Because on Valentine's Day, it seems that the whole universe of people happily engaged, married or in any other way coupled, conspire against you and your inevitable, depressing and unhealthy loneliness.

Giles

From the mess I hear at the door when he fumbles to find the keys in his backpack, I know Michael will be home in a few seconds. The ground floor of our building is occupied by an English school which also holds evening classes, so we often find the main entrance already open.

I try to recompose myself and provide an apparently calm expression.

'Fuck!' Yes, it's really him. There are no more doubts now, indeed.

I pretend to look for a beer in the fridge. I'm really looking for it, in fact. As I turn around, Michael gives me a sulky look. Not that his typical expression is usually any different.

We are not remarkably alike. Apart from the eyes, we both have green. But it's due to chance because our kinship is still quite distant.

I turn around with the beer bottle and close the fridge while Michael throws his jacket on the couch.

'Shitty day?' I ask him, simulating indifference. A shitty day is a rule for us; it falls within our standards. What happened to me, however, is not. It comes dangerously close to disaster.

'I risk fucking losing my second job! That bitch will take advantage of it to kick me out!'

I don't understand what the bitch would take advantage of. However, Michael's second job is... how can I say... well, I'll just say it. Michael is a kind of entertainer for lonely ladies. As I understood, the lonely ladies rent him for the necessary time, maybe until they overcome the solitude. As if it was a disease and Michael was the remedy. The bitch he talks about instead is...

'Damned Miranda Crossing!' Michael sits on the couch and then stands up with an almost catlike movement. He reaches me, opens the fridge, and takes a beer. 'You know she hates me, that bitch!'

'That she hates you, I know, you practically repeat it daily...' I nod and move to let him pass. 'But why should she kick you

15

out? As far as I know, you are an indispensable source of income for her.'

'That ugly...' Michael quivers, biting his lips. Miranda Crossing can be defined in the most varied and picturesque ways, but she certainly isn't ugly. I saw her only once in passing, but it was enough for me to realize it. 'In short, she tells me: "You have the onset of a cold or flu, it seems to me. You know we can't afford collateral damage, can we? You know that you absolutely can't make our clients ill?"' Michael clumsily imitates Miranda's very British voice and accent, which I don't personally know anyway. So, I can't judge his interpretation.

'How did she realize that you have the onset of a cold or flu? And anyway, here currently, everyone has the onset of a cold or flu... all of Ireland has the onset of a cold or flu, if not worse!'

'Actually, she is not wrong; I feel it coming...' Michael grimaces, sips his beer, and then moves back to the couch. 'And I really didn't need it at this moment. I must try to stop it by any means!'

'You can always ask for sick leave, like all ordinary human beings.' I shrug my shoulders and join him. I don't feel like comforting him. At least he has a job. Indeed, two, if we consider the less profitable but official one, as well.

'But I'm not an ordinary human being. And Miranda is not a sympathetic boss. She is a money machine, that woman. She's greedy and merciless, a kind of cyborg.' Michael runs his hands through his dark hair and purses his lips. 'I have to shake it off!' He looks at me with the expression of a rattlesnake, ready to swallow the prey. He also tightens his eyes, pointing at me.

'And to get over it, are you thinking of giving it to me as a gift?' I leave promptly. 'Stay away from me, don't even think about sneezing on me! Don't pass me your virus; I'm already a loser enough myself. I don't need that as well.'

'Too bad you're not a pretty girl, otherwise...' he wrinkles his nose with an almost evil grin. 'In fact, it wouldn't be a bad idea.'

16

'Tell me you're not thinking of making out with someone just for...' I roll my eyes and shake my head. 'There's no guarantee that it works, anyway.'

'I've nothing to lose by trying.'

'Unless you find one who looks even worse than you.'

'Oh, fuck...' He stretches his legs and fusses on the couch. He snorts and shakes his head resentfully. 'Never trust women. But I could actually take sick leave if...'

'You just said the bitch would kick you out...'

'Yes, she would certainly do it. Unless I found her a temporary substitute until I can get back in great shape.'

'Yes, it could be an idea,' I nod unconvincingly.

Who in the world would accept to become a kind of temporary toy boy waiting for the return of the official toy boy?

'You could do it! You earn pittance or just a little more with your job; you might need a little extra for a while.'

No. I won't even earn that pittance anymore. But Michael can't know.

'I already had you leave the leaflets at the Trasks a few weeks ago, mixed with the other advertising they have on the counter. Which moreover...' Moreover, I also lost my job at the Trasks. But no, I could never fall so low. I'm not a gigolo. I'm not a toy boy or prostitute or... I mean, no. Then Michael knows how to deal with women; I don't! Not that way, at least.

'Which, moreover... are they still there?' Michael ends the sentence for me without suspecting that there is something else in my mind instead. 'Didn't your boss catch them yet? Maybe his wife might be interested. The poor woman seems unsatisfied. There's a special offer for Valentine's Day. Miranda hates Valentine's Day; she would eradicate the whole day from the calendar if she could. She would eradicate Christmas as well. And while she is at it, the whole of humanity, too; why not? But Valentine's Day, in terms of profits, always pays her well!'

17

'Yes, they're still there.' Those fucking flyers that offer a ladies' chaperone willing to do anything are still there. I'm not, however. Maybe I should try to mention something. 'The problem is that I…'

'Valentine's Day is the time of the year she targets the most, the bitch. The fulcrum in which much of the work is concentrated and more demanding in the organisation. And then there is also that stupid annual party…'

Clearly, Michael has no understanding or even empathy qualities. He interrupts me without worrying about what I might have to say. Every sentence brings him back to the bitch Miranda Crossing all the time.

Someone who carries on an agency that deals with finding male companionship for alone women must have some problems already. Nothing exaggerated. They don't go further, although I honestly am unconvinced about it. It's against Miranda's rules, according to Michael. I think he talks a load of bullshit.

'I lost my job at the Trasks.' Here, I said it, and that's it. At least I won't be forced to put up with the frustrating selfishness of my pseudo-cousin.

In fact, he freezes. He pushes the beer bottle away from his lips and looks at me, confused. I could have made him stop talking about himself, the absurd Miranda Crossing's agency… and Miranda Crossing.

'What have you done?'

'Hmm…' I'm looking for an effective way to synthesise. 'Gerrit Trask thought I was messing about with his wife.'

'And you weren't?' A sarcastic smile is painted on Michael's face.

'Obviously not. There was only a misunderstanding, let's say.'

I avoid telling him how the facts actually happened. The amused expression he's giving me makes me want to kick his ass already.

'So, you're completely free! You can seize the chance; it would be a great opportunity.' He grins, shrugging his shoulders. 'At the beginning, I was sceptical too. If it wasn't for Stephen...'

Stephen Alden is a guy who has been attending Michael's public relations and internet marketing courses for years, as well as the same gym. The excessive care of his body had appeared strange to Michael, exaggerated more than anything. So, Stephen turned out to be what he is... or was; this still needs to be clarified. A staff member of Miranda. Now, he seems willing to leave that to dedicate himself to something more profitable.

'No, I thank you for the courtesy of temporarily taking your place, but... no, really. I just don't think prostituting myself for some unsatisfied clients is what I want to do.'

'It's not just about that, you know. In fact, it's not about that at all.'

Yes, I know. As I knew that Michael would have taken the opportunity to reiterate the true nature of his employment with the agency "Secret Agents at Your Service". And that ruling, apparently, they need to sign to become part of it as employees. It's absolutely forbidden to go to bed with clients.

'But if you find them pretty, what do you do?' I take it as a game; there is no other way to restore my situation by now.

'Especially if they're pretty, they should be avoided from that point of view. They could bring trouble.'

'It sounds easy, but...' I sigh and let myself fall on the couch. I'm tired. And I'm afraid I feel a cold coming on me as well.

'Of course, you could even do it to get some extra money.' Michael strokes his chin and looks seriously meditating on it. 'Obviously, the bitch wouldn't like it if she finds out.'

'It seemed to me that you said you would never go that far...'

'I just answered you. You raised the issue of what to do if the clients are pretty.' He yawns, stretches, and folds his arms behind his head. 'Actually, what Stephen does is much better, no personal complication, no contact... unless he decides to have it, total independence.'

He's seriously thinking about it. Not so much about contravening Miranda's rules but about what Stephen does as a cam boy, or what the hell it's called. Sexy webcam shows and a specialised website for online promotion, as I understood.

'So, you're thinking about it?'

'No, not at all. As soon as I finish my master's degree, I think I'll leave. America, maybe. Or I'll return to England, I don't know yet.'

'Yes, I understand you. Me too...' I shrug my shoulders and shake my head. I should resume my interrupted studies. I felt like a failure when I left the university imposed on me by my father.

No, there is no "me too". I'm out of options because I don't know where else to go. And without a job. The only chance for me is to go home. Despite not having any desire and my stomach turns at the mere idea. Maybe not to New York and not even in New Jersey. Despite the promise that my grandfather took from me. So, without having found my roots and without even having looked for them very actively.

What alternatives have I left? Going to look for another sad and underpaid job. Waiting for something better without knowing exactly when it will happen. Or... accept Michael's offer and take his place in that strange agency of ladies' chaperones so that I don't waste time and can earn something in these coming weeks. While I'm looking and waiting for a more suitable and, above all, less embarrassing job.

CHAPTER 3

Julie

When I accepted to work as an assistant for Sarah Ward, I should have imagined that she mostly meant "assigned to whatever task and duty happens at any time of the day or even at night, if possible." All around-assistant, in short. Also, babysitter. Especially babysitter. And indeed, it's useless to deny it. I had imagined it.

Sarah is a reasonably well-known chef and food blogger in the city. And I really want to follow her path. This is why I immediately accepted the job without blinking an eye at her requests. I met her at one of my first cooking classes in Dublin. It was a course on spices that I don't think I will ever particularly need; I chose it because it was the cheapest on the list. But at least I met Sarah, who, with her advice, will help me take the first steps to enter that environment.

Now, among other things, I have been tasked with collecting her favourite laptop in her trusted store in the Jervis Shopping Centre area. She has four other computers in her house. Her husband's and one desktop. Plus, two spare laptops that she uses occasionally. But apparently, without her favourite, she can't think, she can't write, and she feels uncomfortable. Even the recipes come out wrong. All right, so... yes, in short, it's understandable. Or maybe she overstated the issue on purpose to send me here in her place while she was busy preparing a radio interview.

Everything would have been fine if I hadn't been forced to bring Sarah's three children along, two boys and a girl between three and seven, Charlie, Anthony, and Mandy. They are not three normal children but three little out-of-control brats who cannot be looked after simultaneously. They seem determined to make trouble. Indeed, they don't seem. They are actually determined. They appear as three smiling little angels with typical Irish red hair and blue eyes; only the halo around their little heads missing. But the truth is another thing.

It's a nightmare to walk down a city centre street with them. Especially if it's an almost constantly crowded street like Henry Street. Fortunately, it's a pedestrian street, and there are no cars to avoid. They see shops, and they each escape in different directions. And they want to have everything. They're without restraint. At first, I tried to please them. I believed that the children's benevolence would help me achieve my goal. Now I understand that it won't, and it won't work like that. They are little dictators, cruel and spoiled. Not even Sarah can control them most of the time. And she complains about their insolence attributing the blame to her husband, who, in turn, blames her for not teaching the children proper manners.

We had to take the bus, although it wouldn't have taken too long to get here on foot. The youngest refused to walk and wanted to be carried in my arms. The other two pouted, claiming that they were tired too.

I must be strong and endure. Work for the cause. Okay, all right, I must keep my main goal in mind. Become like Sarah, a famous chef and food blogger. This will guarantee me a bright future and, above all, to be well paid. Chefs and food bloggers are the new stars; I would never be out of work! Because everyone, everyone really likes to eat well. Many people are interested in food and cooking. One day, they could even let me have my own TV show... or on the radio, like Sarah.

Then, besides having Sarah on my side, I could win over Kate Norman's sympathies. She occasionally teaches the dessert class I'm attending, and I participated in her demonstration conference. Her lessons are costly, but I'm saving to be able to join her famous vegetable course. Once I show my talent to Kate, I'll be well on my way to achieving my goal!

I arrive in front of the shop Sarah pointed me to, "Trask Electric", on the corner of Henry Street and a small side street past Arnotts, near the Jervis Shopping Centre. I walk in and look around; it seems strangely deserted compared to the other shops on the main road. The lady owner was a high school friend of Sarah. I dragged the three brats, to whom I was forced to buy ice cream, from the Italian ice cream shop located along that street. I can't understand how they feel like having ice cream in this cold. As soon as they enter, they disperse into the shop, each running in a different direction, as expected. I'm sure about it by now. They decide to drive crazy anyone in charge of looking after them.

I see an elegant woman coming towards me in a dark blue suit and with her hair gathered. She wears two large hoop earrings that catch my attention.

'Good morning; I'm here to pick up Sarah Ward's laptop. She told me it would be ready today.'

I studied my sentence by heart in English, as I always do when I have to face people I don't know, and I can prepare myself in advance. I don't like showing my French accent blatantly and try to mask it as much as possible.

'Oh, damn it, it's true!' The woman replies with an irritated, almost hostile tone and attitude that clash with the elegance of her appearance. 'No, don't be afraid. That's not meant for you. I remember promising Sarah two days ago, but... my husband had the brilliant idea of firing our assistant technician, who should have taken care of it yesterday. Or try, at least. So, it's not ready yet.'

Bad news. Now I'll have to study a sentence to tell Sarah about it. Unless I ask this kind lady to explain to her friend the problems arising from the dismissal of their assistant technician.

In short, I must find a way not to get involved in that mess. Sarah needs to update her blog by tomorrow, and she is already stressed out because she fears not receiving enough comments and views compared to her fiercer rivals, Jessica Summers and Nattie Washburn. She must update the blog with her computer because she can't work well with others and needs more time to get used to them. It could take her days or weeks that she doesn't have at her disposal. This is what she constantly repeats.

If I bring her this news, she will pick on anyone within her reach, as she always does when she's nervous. In this case, on me, specifically. Without forgetting that, to blow off some steam on her own, she will surely force me to take care of the three brats beyond the established time. And I'll also have to take them somewhere, again, because she refuses to have them around in those moments. Not to damage their balance with her frustration and emotional tension, being the overly busy mother she is. It's what she always says. But I fear that the "damage" has already been underway. From birth, perhaps.

'Could you explain the situation to Sarah?' I timidly suggest to the woman, who, of course, pretends not to hear me.

She turns towards a man who has just arrived from a door leading to the store's back.

'I told you; you shouldn't have sacked him!' She assaults him. 'What do we do now?'

The man frowns, turns his gaze to me, and then back to the woman. I guess he's her husband. The one who got me into trouble, in fact. He has a merry but unhappy appearance at the same time. He scratches his nape with one hand noisily. While waiting, I glance around to avoid losing Sarah's three children, in addition to her computer not being ready for collection. They are chasing each other among the washing machines. I hope they avoid ventures into areas where they can knock over or break something. I don't call them to order because I know, from experience, that scolding them and telling them not to do something is the best way to get them to do it.

'Now I'll take care of it; I've always taken care of it!' Even the man's tone is not very conciliatory. They excluded me from the conversation about the computer I should collect as if I wasn't there. As if I wasn't a highly valued customer. Maybe they only consider me the maid of a highly valued customer.

I sigh and lean against the counter; I feel exhausted. The woman gives an impatient glance; I wonder if towards me or her husband. Then, she changes and becomes supportive, almost understanding. She nods to me to wait and follows her husband in the back.

I get distracted by the various advertising flyers piled on the counter. "Cuban Dance Course" Oh wow, maybe I should move my bottom a little with some Cuban guy... "Learn Irish with us" would then be Gaelic, which usually drives me crazy on buses, and I'm only finally getting used to it now... "We manufacture beautiful and elegant pillows with your old curtains." ... But why, if someone wants a pillow, doesn't buy one directly?... "Indian cooking course". This could be useful to me, maybe some basics. I lift the flyer and decide to put it in my bag.

But my gaze is caught by another one below the Indian cuisine that now emerges halfway through. I can make out the word "Valent...". I move the other flyers and read in full: "Secret Agents at Your Service" Agency. A little further down: *"Rent a Secret Agent for Valentine's Day"* on a red background with the silhouette of a man in a suit and bow tie, who might vaguely resemble James Bond. Further down, *"Why not live a fairytale week with a man who venerates you and makes you feel like the most beautiful and desired woman on the love feast?"*

25

Giles

After talking with Michael, I spent the evening updating my resume and looking for job offers online. This morning, I woke up early to continue the venture. It won't be easy and will take time, I realize that. The one with the Trasks was only a temporary job, even though I have excellent knowledge of computer science and I know how to repair appliances. Thanks to my granddad, who dragged me with him as a boy, paying me weekly pocket money. Plus, I work well with computers too; usually, when I get my hands on them, I can get them to start working again. I have the magic touch.

But my real job is as a financial advisor. Or at least it should be, even if I need to catch up to achieve an adequate specialisation. Certainly, in the meantime, I have no intention of asking my father for money, who would like me to return to his employment in the family business that produces gardening tools. I could take care of the commercial and financial sectors of the company, of course. And I would be forced to finish the university that my father chose for me. At this point, I prefer to continue my studies here. But the truth is that I still have doubts that it's really the right job for me, so if I depended on my father, I would no longer have a choice. I should bend to my fate, whether I like it or not.

So, what's left for me to do? Accept Michael's indecent proposal? Or go back to the Trasks and explain to Gerrit that it was an accident, a misunderstanding? When they hired me, the guy who worked for them before me had just left. And the truth is that, despite Annette's goodwill, Gerrit cannot deal with customers; he doesn't know how to interact with them and scares them with his attitude. He manages to be fair in accounting and is almost brilliant in pulling off favourable prices from suppliers, often after offering them a beer and some healthy discussion about the latest rugby matches.

I close my laptop, grab my jacket, and run down the stairs. I move towards Henry Street, only a few minutes from my apartment in Parnell Street. With every step, I feel more furious. I really didn't do anything with Annette. Maybe I could have brought that stupid bracelet with me and seized the chance to return it since, in the meantime, I managed to release it from the zip of my jeans. I think of returning home to get it. But it's better to leave it where it is, forget about it and not enrage Gerrit's angry horned man's instinct.

I arrive on Henry Street and, after walking a short distance, I turn the corner and find myself in front of the Trasks' shop. I hold my breath momentarily, reflecting that it's better to abandon that drifting couple to its destiny. Trying to provide or demand explanations is useless; discussing with someone I already know won't listen.

But I'm here now! What the hell! I throw myself into the shop as if throwing myself into a battle to the death. Unexpectedly, my vehemence is stemmed and blocked as soon as I cross the threshold. I am hit by three red-haired kids looking sullenly up at me. Immediately behind them, their mother seems to have the pissed-off expression of someone who would like to abandon them anywhere so as not to drag them along.

'I mean, be careful...' she sighs and looks hostile. I almost suspect she is turning to me, too. Then she looks down at the youngest of the three. 'Anthony, be careful with that ice cream. If you don't want it anymore, just say it, but don't throw it around!'

Instead, the little demon really throws it around. And he throws it right towards me, with the defiant expression of someone who has done it intentionally, too! What a coincidence; it ends right there. I can really say that I have got fucking problems in this place! Obviously, all objects, people and foods are attracted to "it"!

'Oh...' the woman looks down. Right there, too. And she stares with a shocked expression. As if instead of having my jeans stained with ice cream, it had just come out of my pants in her presence.

'I mean, madam... couldn't you look after your kids?' I realize it's probably not her fault, but I don't know who else to take it on and feel embarrassed.

'I...' The woman doesn't seem to know how to respond. I noticed an accent in the sentences she pronounced, but I couldn't identify it. She looks embarrassed but looks up at me instead. Now, she seems more enraged, actually. So much so that I don't know whether to apologise or get even more pissed off. I lose myself a little looking at her face, flushed cheeks, and blue eyes.

Meanwhile, she opens her bag and looks for something inside. She hands me some paper handkerchiefs and gives me the umpteenth impatient look. Before I can say anything, she has already rushed to the exit to pursue her three devilish kids.

Nothing left for me but to try to clean up the damage with the handkerchiefs I found in my hand. I thought it was worse; I easily clean the vanilla ice cream layer and try to hide the stain by pulling down my sweater. Why does this always happen to me?

'So... here again.' Annette's voice distracts me from my deed. She partly closes her eyes with an intentionally seductive expression. 'You decided to pick up where we left off, as far as I can see.'

'It's not a game, Mrs. Trask.' I voluntarily force the detachment. I have always called her Annette without having to stand on ceremonies, and our conversations have always been very confidential. Maybe I shouldn't have let her think that I'd been interested in her. 'I'm not having fun, and I'm not back here to get in trouble. I told you clearly that I'm not interested. But I would like to talk, and I deserve an explanation... in fact, there is no explanation. You can't...'

'You bet I can!' Gerrit emerges; I don't know where from. Not from the back because I didn't see him coming from there. 'Get out of here, take your shit with you and don't come back ever again! If you keep bothering my wife, I'll call the Guards!'

He moves behind the counter as he speaks and lowers himself to get something. From the trash can, that's right at that point.

I find some crumpled leaflets of Michael in my hand. I don't understand the connection, and I don't understand what they have to do with me and our situation.

'Get lost!' He orders me furiously. I'm afraid he's thinking of pouncing on me with all his weight if I don't obey.

Annette watches me with an unhappy and, at the same time, irritated expression but doesn't intervene. Her silence confirms her husband's decision, even though she seemed to have a different opinion earlier.

There is nothing left for me to do but leave. I find myself outside, for the second time, with the damned leaflets in my hands. I sigh and shake my head. Inevitably, I find myself reading the invitation to hire a secret agent for Valentine's Day.

No, I can't believe it. Or I don't want to think about it yet; I refuse to consider the possibility and think that it could be a good source of immediate income, what I need most at the moment. Because I tremble at the idea that one of these elusive agents could be me.

CHAPTER 4

Julie

Finally arrived at Sarah's house, I will now be forced to face her. Fortunately, she hasn't arrived yet, so I can take some time to organise my ideas.

I can't believe I did it. In short, I felt like a thief even though I tried to act secretly and stealthily. I held one of the Trasks' flyers and slipped it into my bag. Nothing serious or illegal, at least for me. However, it wasn't the one concerning cooking but... the other.

Meanwhile, the two owners continued their discussion animatedly. Annette, I caught her name while she was arguing with her husband, moved towards me to explain the actual problem. They have no one to repair the computer, but she promises to fix everything within a day or two.

What could I say facing the inevitable? I thanked them and called the children to order, preparing for the big exit.

'What the fuck are these?' Apparently, the Valentine's Day flyers, which remained on display on the white counter, attracted the attention of her husband, whose name could be Gerry, Garrit, or something like that.

'Oh, they must be from that friend of Giles who passed by a few days ago... in fact, he's his cousin, I think.' Annette glanced at her husband halfway between sadistic and threatening, snatching one of the flyers from his hand. 'Interesting!'

'I never gave him permission to leave them here!' Her husband raised his voice, almost yelling.

'But I did!' Obviously, his wife didn't give up. She almost seemed to enjoy the confrontation.

As I turned around, after trying in vain to intrude on the conversation to clarify my requests and remind them of the problem with Sarah's laptop, I resigned but found myself unable to leave. To finish instead, almost up against an annoyed-looking guy who stood at the entrance. And who complained, mistaking me for the mother of the three little brats. When Anthony crashed into him with the ice cream and stained his jeans just at the height of... I didn't know whether to feel embarrassed or laugh in his face. I handed him some tissues and cleared out with the excuse of running after the children. Maybe I should have offered to pay for the dry cleaners... I was rude. But he would have taken off his trousers and... No, perhaps I should have gotten the bill sent to me. Well, it went like this for now. I ran away.

In any case, this matter of the Valentine's Day chaperone seems really sad to me, just for poor, desperate women. Almost worse than the single party that usually takes place the next day. Waiting for Sarah, I'm turning the stupid flyer over in my hands. The three brats stop, fortunately in silence, in front of a cartoon on TV. It won't last long, I know. They have the incredible ability to get tired of a game or program within five or, at most, ten minutes at best. Sooner or later, one of the three will start to get bored and complain, distracting the other two.

Anyway, no. I could never organise such a thing for Valerie. It really would be a too absurd situation. If it happened to me, I'd feel ridiculous, not... how does it say...? I resume the flyer. Oh, here... *"the most beautiful and desired woman."*

I take advantage of the apparent calm at home to make a phone call just to Valerie. She answers me with a barely perceptible voice and sniffling. I don't know if she has caught a cold or is crying again. At this point, I really hope it's a cold.

'Hi, I'm still at Sarah's.' I'd like to entertain her to help her think less about what happened to her. 'If you want, we can go out when I get back.'

'No, Julie. Thanks for the thought, but I'm tired, really...' she sighs deeply. She seems really distressed. 'I feel exhausted today. Once at home, I will go straight to bed. I have this chronic sore throat that doesn't want to pass.'

'All right then, I'll see you later.'

Valerie moved to Dublin for Trent, mainly. She didn't have other reasons. They had met in France, where she taught French conversation in a school for foreigners. The students' French level was intermediate to high, so for Valerie, there was no need for an excellent knowledge of English or other languages to hold her course.

Now that the relationship is over, Valerie has realized she is not doing well here. Because of the bad weather, she fell ill several times last year. She would like to move to the Canary Islands or a place with milder weather. Anyway, if she has to work as a waitress or a sales assistant because her English is not good enough, it's useless to stay. At this point, a warm place is better, with more sun and less rain. And then, as she says, her Spanish is better than her English.

I got sick, too. Too many times compared to my usual average. I'm trying to fight the cough that's slowly advancing. I already had it in November, and now it seems intent on getting back even fiercer. But I believe disappointment made her sick as far as Valerie is concerned. We may need some healthy fun. Then, we could even leave and move to the Canary Islands. But I want to finish the courses I started here and try to assert myself as a chef and, above all, as a food blogger. Later I can work anywhere, from any other place, country, island, or universe.

Essentially, now, I need money to pay for my courses. Especially those held by Kate Norman. I close my eyes for a moment, almost forcing myself to think. I open them again like crossed by a flash. A flash of genius, to be precise. I look again for the flyer I've found in that shabby and mismanaged appliance store. I'm struck by a sensational idea. Who knows, they might even hire women to do this job.

Giles

I give up. The attempt with the Trasks had a tragic outcome, and I will never show up again. However, I must find an alternative and a good idea to make money immediately. It seems that the ideal solution is right in front of my eyes. I look down at the damn flyer as I bite the ham sandwich I've made as soon as I got back home.

Michael assured me that they wouldn't expect me to sleep with clients. Indeed, it's expressly forbidden by the rules. It would be helpful for me to put something aside while looking for a proper and more appropriate job. Of course, it is not sure that Miranda Crossing even wants to hire me as one of her "agents".

Lying on the couch, I wait impatiently for Michael to come home in the evening to return to the conversation.

'I couldn't get the job back with the Trasks...'

It's the first thing I say when he enters the front door and has yet to reach the living room.

'Of course, you shouldn't have got off with the boss's wife. Especially not under his nose.'

'I didn't get off with her!' I rebel against his bored tone, unmoved by my misfortunes.

'Then you didn't have to "didn't get off with her" under his nose!' He yawns loudly and stretches right before me. 'You know what they say... out of sight, out of mind.'

'Yes, I know. But now...' I snort, shrugging my shoulders. I'm looking for the right way to face the subject. I just face it. There is no right way, and Michael certainly doesn't give a damn about half-measures. 'Is yesterday's offer still valid, or did you find someone else? And in any case... are they hiring?'

'I can arrange an appointment with Miranda if you're not afraid of being torn to pieces.' Michael gives me an indifferent look and walks over to the fridge. 'You still have to pass under her, even if you temporarily take my place.'

'You mean...' No, he doesn't mean that. He can't. Even if he gives me that look like he implies literally "under her".

'Of course, she intends to test the goods firsthand.'

I wasn't wrong. He's fucking serious. So, just to be clear, I'm about to go from the frying pan to the fire.

'If... there is no other choice...'

Michael uncorks the beer and sips it eagerly.

'You're so naïve, Giles. That's why they'll always fuck you up in life.'

Oh, thank you! I really needed someone to throw the truth to my face! I don't reply; I'm holding back from telling him to go to hell. I cross my arms, and I suddenly desire to go out. I'll probably walk into the first pub I come across to get myself a beer accompanied by a healthy chat with the first stranger who will sit next to me. Soon, they will all be talking about the Six Nations rugby tournament.

'I was kidding, of course!' Michael rolls his eyes and sighs. 'Forget about it; that shrew won't let anybody touch her, not even with a feather!'

'Oh, great! Thanks for taking the piss out of me!' I get up anyway, and now I'm launched. 'But she didn't seem so much a shrew... I might... you know...'

'Don't be a jerk now!' Michael strangely shows signs of impatience. Yet the one pissed off should be me at this point. 'Do you want it or not, the appointment with the bitch?'

CHAPTER 5

Julie

The days are inexorably passing, and the fateful date is approaching. I don't know how to avoid it with Valerie. Now, it's no longer just about Valentine's Day and all my unfortunate relationships that were wrecked just nearing that wretched feast of love. It will also coincide with Valerie's not-a-wedding day.

We meet for lunch; I am still trying to figure out what to talk to her about. We are both on our break. She is from the fast-food chain where she works; I am from Sarah's children, who are busy with their afternoon activities. Fortunately, I have not suffered direct repercussions due to the failure to collect her favourite laptop.

I'm tempted to mention something to Val about that bizarre agency. You know, just for a laugh. But it seems too risky a move. It is better to totally change the subject and reply to one of her comments about work.

'I'm sure you'll find something better soon. Your English is progressing considerably.' Considerably is too much. But Val needs encouragement. 'I've seen that they're looking for staff in the Irish souvenir shop in Grafton Street, the nice one where we bought bags, T-shirts, and traditional music CDs. Even in Temple Bar, some clothing stores are looking. Better than fast food, don't you think?'

'Thank you, Julie. But I don't worry too much now...' she sighs, carefully pouring the dressing on her salad. 'I'm almost convinced to go home, and then I'll decide where to go from there. I would have already done it if it wasn't too shameful a feeling.'

'You have nothing to be ashamed of, Val...' I sigh and lean my fork on the plate instead of bringing the piece of pizza to my mouth.

'I know, but with friends... I mean, I left town as if I was going to conquer the world...' she sighs and shakes her head. 'Instead, I ended up doing a job I hate because I can't get anything better. And my boyfriend, after asking me to marry him and announcing it to the world, dumped me. He no longer felt ready. I planned to travel the world with him. We planned it together. Little by little, obviously, as we were both working...'

'Was that really what you wanted? Or what he wanted?' I don't know where my question arose, but it came out by now. We have examined the subject in every way in the last few weeks. Discussing Trent's reasons and Val's non-existent faults and failings. But we never talked about this. Did she really want a life beside him? Trying to meet his needs? Moving to his country? Accepting a job that doesn't excite her?

'The truth is, I don't know, Julie. I don't know anymore. I know I wanted him, so everything else would have been fine for me.'

Valerie's answer doesn't surprise me. I saw her together with Trent. But that's what happens when you fall in love. Anything is fine. We adapt to any situation.

'Why don't you try looking for the same job you had in France? You could teach French here as well.' I completely change the subject; better that than to pile on too much emphasis on her feelings for Trent. Even though it was at a French course for foreigners that they met, so I don't know how much my attempt can serve to distract her.

'I don't know, maybe...' Valerie shrugs and then stares back at her salad with a very absorbed expression.

She seems indifferent now to what happens to her here. Despite my encouragement, she may be thinking about leaving and concentrating all her interests elsewhere because, obviously, there is nothing left to keep her in Dublin. Nothing and nobody. Me neither.

But this means that I will be alone. With superficial connections in this city, nothing more. I'm afraid I must resign myself to the idea while waiting for something to change.

As I think about what to say to break the silence, my cell phone on the table rings. I see the name Trask appearing, and suddenly, I remember leaving my number and e-mail address with the lady in the middle of our discussion.

I answer, and it's really her, Annette Trask. She tells me that the computer will be ready soon. She apologises for the inconvenience caused and concludes by saying I will hear from her as soon as possible, maybe even later today.

I hang up and try to resume the conversation with Valerie, using the phone call I just received to explain what happened and change the subject. Valerie nods without looking particularly interested.

'What do you intend to do?' She finally asks me, staring at me with her clear eyes.

'I will go and get it as soon as it's ready; I will get rid of the problem at least. If it's today, it's even better!'

'I didn't mean that.' She pulls the plate away and rests her elbows on the table, interlacing her fingers. She leans forward towards me as if to look at me better. 'In your life, Julie. What do you intend to do?'

37

Giles

I accepted it almost as a joke, but the matter became damn serious. And really, Michael set me up for an appointment with the infamous Miranda Crossing. The agency is located in the Finglas area. I've only been there a couple of times with Michael. Once in a pub, the other to return a car we had rented. I must be careful to avoid ending up lost.

Fortunately, I can identify the building where the agency is located, in a slightly off-centre area of Finglas Village. After passing a bank and a supermarket, I walk along a little less travelled road. It was well hidden. And there is no sign, only the name "M. Crossing" on the bell. I ring, I introduce myself, and they open it for me.

I climb two flights of stairs to reach it. The interior smells old, but I am still in the shared common space; I have yet to reach the real entrance of the agency.

When I get there, I ring another bell and wait. It's she in person who opens the door for me. And she's more beautiful than I remembered, after only seeing her briefly when I went to the pub with Michael. She keeps her dark hair partly gathered while some strands fall on her shoulders. And she stares into my eyes as if challenging me while she tilts her face slightly.

With a nod of her head, she invites me to enter and then to follow her along the corridor. I can't help staring at her body as she precedes me. Her slim figure and rounded shapes are in the right places; despite wearing dark grey trousers and a jacket suit that looks like a hymn to sobriety, everything in her cries sensuality and ardour.

I'm exaggerating, I know. It may be her job that makes me perceive a distorted image. Or maybe Michael's contempt suddenly seems too exaggerated to me.

We sit in her office, as modest and sober as she is. It seems to reflect her image. Dark desk and two very minimalist chairs in front. Her chair on the other side is similar. A painting on the wall characterises one of Picasso's cubism periods. I'm not an expert, but it's the one in which he represented pieces of a woman, mixing their features. Not far away is a light green sofa that looks uncomfortable, almost without a backrest.

I look around so as not to point my eyes directly at her; she looks at me as if waiting for my misstep even though I have just entered, and we haven't started discussing anything about the job she might offer me. But then, inevitably, I'm called to order and forced to look at her as she talks to me.

'So, you're Michael Wrighton's cousin. I guess he has already explained to you something about how things work here.' Her voice is sweeter and more caressing than I imagined, and despite her attractiveness, it clashes with the woman's cold and detached image.

'Yes, I would say he already explained everything to me, madam.'

I try to take the most professional attitude possible. I dressed up, too, although I now feel like a mannequin. White shirt, blue suit, and tie. I must be able to resist until the end. At least until I convince this woman to give me the job and pay me well. Then, I'll manage when I'm dealing directly with the clients, somehow.

'So, you will know that intimate relationships with the ladies requesting our services are absolutely forbidden, even if they declare they are willing to pay a few extras for that purpose. Is that clear to you, Mr. McGrath?'

Clear. Limpid. Crystal clear. I won't become a prostitute; relax, my dear ice woman. I don't answer that way, of course.

'Sure, Mrs. Crossing.'

'And, of course, no contact other than those established through the agency. No attempt to... how to say, to make single women of a certain age and perhaps in possession of a conspicuous inheritance fall in love.'

But what does she think I am, this woman? I feel blushing, and I'd like to jump on her. Is she calling me... in short, what do they say for men? The term escapes me, but it should exist. I run my hand over my forehead. I feel humiliated, and in my life, I have never felt so much solidarity with the female universe when it is accused of such actions.

On the other hand, she very composedly doesn't care about my state of mind. She stares at me with her dark eyes and looks more and more like an eagle, ready to lash out at its prey to tear it to pieces. And yet... she said nothing different from what Michael had already explained to me. But her way... her composure... the contemptuous expression she is staring at me now. Despite her beautiful face and the two slightly lighter hair strands that come down to caress her cheeks, this woman no longer arouses in me any attraction compared to the initial impact. I just want to run away, to stay away from her.

'I don't...' I realize that I will have to answer something sooner or later. 'I don't intend to aim at anyone's inheritance...'

I almost preferred to go back and beg the Trasks. Or any other job would have been fine for me. What the hell came into my mind? And how can Michael suffer all this?

'Expenses are obviously charged to the agency. In fact, your only task will be to behave like a gentleman with the ladies and make them feel good in your company. Do you think you can do it?'

Michael was right. Even her overly British accent starts to get on my nerves. Now is she accusing me of being an American bumpkin who doesn't know how to behave with ladies?

'I know how to behave like a perfect gentleman with the ladies! You have no idea what I can do!' I reply, perhaps a little too much in kind this time.

She tilts her head slightly and gives me a contemptuous look.

'Oh really? And what can you do? Let's hear it.'

'I can be a gentleman, of course. Make a woman feel wanted, loved...' But what the fuck am I saying? When did I ever!

'We agreed a little while ago that you absolutely shouldn't deceive and make a woman fall in love with you. And do you know why, Mr. McGrath?' She doesn't expect an answer, so I don't even try. She wants to teach me a lesson. She has the typical attitude of a schoolteacher who reproaches a somewhat idiotic student. 'Because a client in love, especially of a certain age, is a client who is most often not returned. And do you know what becomes of a client who believes she has been deluded and feels not reciprocated, Mr. McGrath? A pissed-off client, unhappy with the service and willing to create great trouble. The kind of trouble I will have to solve, not you.'

I lose myself trying to understand if she really pronounced the word "pissed-off" in the middle of her monologue. Because even a bad word seems to lose the desired effect on this woman's lips. Inviting but stone lips, like everything else. Or icy lips. In any case, dangerous lips. On second thoughts, she might even bite.

'I understand it all, Mrs. Crossing. Gentleman but without sex and love.' A mannequin, in short. But are there women who really rent a mannequin?

'Are you thinking that no one in these degenerate modern times would accept a bit of good taste and healthy romance without transcending into a sexual relationship and without having a love relationship as a goal?'

'Yeah, you read my mind, I'm afraid.' I could put my cards on the table because it's clear that I won't win with her. I will never win. 'And anyway... You really know women well.'

'Of course, I'm a woman too.' She raises a smile for the first time. And for the first time, I would have something to say about her statement. There is no doubt that she is a woman. With her heart enclosed in a computer, perhaps, but a woman. 'In any case, men are often not different at all.'

41

'For men, most of the time, it's just about sex, not love. I am a man, I know.' I smile, too; I don't know why. I wanted to pose as a superior being, a man of the world. But now, I mostly feel like an idiot while waiting for Miranda to reply in kind. I expect a memorable offence on her part.

'You're right', she nods slightly, narrowing her eyes. And unexpectedly, she adds nothing else on the subject. She opens a drawer and puts some sheets of paper collected in front of me. 'The weekly pay is the one shown above. So... do you want to sign the agreement, or would you rather let it go?'

'I'll sign the agreement. But I warn you right away that I will be available only for the next few weeks because...' Because I'm in a desperate situation, and I don't want to make too much effort while looking for something else? No, better avoid saying it. Because the weekly pay for five appointments roughly corresponds to what I earned from the Trasks in a month. No, better not to mention to her what my previous salary was.

'Because you want to make easy money while searching for something else.' She gives me a look, which I can't decipher, so I wonder if it's understanding or commiserating. 'What everyone thinks, but who knows why easy money attracts more easy money. And in the end, they all stay at it beyond the time initially planned.'

What does it mean? That everyone ends up trapped? In fact, how long has Michael been working for her? I don't care. It won't happen to me. I need it now. Only a few weeks of easy money without any physical or emotional involvement. I just have to go out with sad, lonely women and behave myself. And the pay is excellent! What more could I wish for?

CHAPTER 6

Miranda

I had already guessed from the first glance that he would accept. I insert his photograph in the file. Very nice, almost perfect features, full lips, green eyes, and light brown hair. Here he is, another toy to add to the collection. Like others before him, he was overflowing with arrogance and lacking common sense. Only for a few weeks, he said. Everyone says that. Many have been with me for years. Michael has been with me for years and is not willing to leave. I'll have to kick him out one of these days.

But the real question is not them; it's obvious why they remained. The real question is me. Why have I "been with me for years"? Why did I continue this nonsense without blinking an eye?

My life was falling apart, and I needed a diversion. Maybe I could have started a crochet or synchronised swimming course instead of agreeing to carry on my Aunt Grace's business. With Aunt Grace's rules, that could have been fine and made sense fifty years ago or even further back, but now it's clear as daylight that no one respects them. Neither the clients nor the "gentlemen" who possibly aim to pocket some easier money. Clear as daylight in Ireland gives more of the idea. Clear only occasionally, then. Clear like a mantle of dark clouds from which an excerpt of blue occasionally peeps out and gives a bit of respite, of hope.

In any case, as that Mr. McGrath kid just said, for men, most of the time, it's just about sex, not love. While women, the poor naïve girls, are deluding themselves to get love through sex. Not all. Some have woken up, luckily for them, and have realized that they have been deceived all their lives by the bedtime fairy tales. Like me.

The truth is that my life was really falling apart, and Aunt Grace and her bizarre activity were like a raft for me to hold on to, trying to stay afloat. My aunt and her friend Janet were two single women who had the idea of trying to make other single women happy. They had nothing in mind compared to what runs on the internet today. They just wanted some company and to be treated well by a man. It seems almost absurd as it may still appear as a utopia for some women, including me.

So, when I became a single woman just like them, I left England to move to Ireland. I just wanted to run away. I never thought it could happen. Aunt Grace was the only relative I had left. My parents had died years before, and my marriage had miserably failed after six years of only illusory happiness.

Actually, this is what it is, I'm afraid. Only illusory happiness for so many couples now. The only difference is that most refuse to admit it. I had also refused to admit it for a long time. Until I had evidence of it in my bed, where I found my ex-husband with his former lover. Immediately after, he promised me to leave her, swearing absolute loyalty from that moment on. But I knew he would never do it. It was clear to me when I told him and his promises to go to hell. Then I didn't talk to him again. He no longer received a single word from me, but only the divorce letter from my lawyer. I subjected him to a war of silence. I've always been the best at that.

I already knew it for months or maybe years. I was just hiding my head in the sand. And it wouldn't even have been necessary to discover a betrayal to understand it.

Something like the agency I ran seems to work for some women. I know that if the circumstances happened to me, it wouldn't work for me. These guys wouldn't work with me.

Maybe because I know it's a pretence. It would only make me aware of being sad, alone, and more frustrated.

Grace and Janet were especially fond of Valentine's Day. They spoke about it as an expression of love in all its forms. I never really understood all their enthusiasm, especially because love seemed to have forgotten them for years. And me, too.

I try to resist the temptation, but then I give up. I do it for myself. To avoid forgetting. I look inside without even lifting the photograph or touching it. It still hurts, but it's precisely how it should be. Even if I denied it, I still believed in it. I was hoping to save something, to save us. Maybe my war of silence has destroyed me even more than shouting all my anger in his face. Now I need it to remember. To make sure that it won't happen again. Never again to me.

I close the drawer with a sudden movement; it produces a slight rumble. I open the one below, and without thinking about it, I grab the box. Chocolate is good for mood, people say. I receive it all the time throughout the year from clients and acquaintances. All they do is give me chocolates, always chocolates. I think I've become addicted now. They may serve to regulate the state of my bitterness.

I must start thinking about the preparations for my party. Another legacy of Aunt Grace. A dinner for Valentine's Day for those with no other possibility, place, or person to celebrate with. A celebration for lonely souls. Maybe it's even more pathetic than the actual feast.

I take a tour of the contents of the files: the boys and the clients. Like I'm rechecking the merchandise before closing everything and going home.

We are in a residential suburb in the north of Dublin. It's not even so easy to find us. Yet they have found us for years. Maybe it continues thanks to Aunt Grace and Janet, even though they are no longer here. Class, refinement, elegance... as if clients had spread the word from the past to the present.

I turn everything off. I get up from my armchair; sooner or later, I'll have to decide to change it because of how uncomfortable it is becoming, but I can't let it go because it was here even before I arrived. I can't say "going home" because I live across the street, in the villa that had always belonged to Aunt Grace and her husband, who died when he was in his early thirties. Although she was a young widow without children, my aunt never remarried. Maybe she could have.

Tomorrow I must decide who to entrust the clients registered for the special Valentine's week. It will begin with the defined phase of "courtship". For me, instead, the stage in which client payments will be deposited in my bank account will begin.

Michael

If he returned home, it means he survived. I don't even want to know how it went. Lately, I've got an idea of Giles. He won't make it, as far as I know him. He will probably return soon to America to be pampered by his family.

'Now I just have to wait for the first date!'

These are the first words he addresses to me, falling heavily on the couch. I'm trying to cook grilled vegetables with awful results. I risk setting everything on fire at this point.

'You mean you managed to get yourself hired?' I can't hide my disbelief.

'Did you have any doubts?' Giles pulls himself together and rests his elbows on his knees. He looks at me with a frown. 'I impressed her. I'm sure. I really hit it off with Miranda.'

'Yes, right, hit it off...' To be honest, his overly self-assured attitude now annoys me. But better to stay silent.

'I notice a certain sarcasm in your way of answering me.'

And he notices well. I can control what I say but not how I say it. Nor the expression with which I say it.

'No, not sarcasm. Just don't let Miranda manipulate you too much.'

'I find her a beautiful woman but also very unhappy.'

Here, I had to imagine it. It's precisely in Giles's nature. What will he do with Miranda? Try to save her from herself and her "unhappiness" by giving her his heart. Too bad for him when he realizes that hers is pure perfidy.

'What do you intend to do with her?' I can't help but ask.

In any case, I won't try to warn him. If Giles has this somewhat lost and dreamy expression, it seems clear to me that Miranda has started with her seduction work. She will tear him to pieces like she did with others before him.

'I have no intentions, but it seems strange that a woman like her is not with someone. I mean... that's my understanding.'

'I think Miranda just doesn't have the right personality to be with someone.' I really think so. And I must admit that in this, we're alike. 'Anyway, you got it right. And I advise you to forget about it, or she won't let you get away with it.'

'Why? Have you been there before, or do you know someone who did?' Giles now stands up and grins as if he has all the answers to that enigma of a woman called Miranda Crossing.

'Let's say I've known her for a few years. No one would come out unharmed, trust me.'

Giles shrugs his shoulders unconvincingly. The conversation stops because he receives a message on his mobile phone.

'Annette Trask...' he reveals to me as if I cared.

I only care about closing the book on Miranda. Even if the first to definitively close the book on Miranda should be really me.

CHAPTER 7

Miranda

Among the questions I will never be able to answer, one of the first just concerns him. He watches me with the expression of someone who knows me well, and in front of his eyes, a little tired but still lively, I end up almost always feeling transparent.

I also asked myself several times why he still allows me to stay. Raymond Murphy, the building owner where I run the "Secret Agents at Your Service" agency, sits right before me. He lives on the first floor and occasionally comes to keep me company. He was a close friend of Aunt Grace and of Janet, a childhood friend of my aunt's husband. He remained alone after his wife's death and his son's move to the United States.

Yes, I wonder why he didn't send me away and didn't think about renting the entire floor. He could get a couple of apartments. Instead, he allows me to use three rooms to run my agency, leaving the others completely empty. When my aunt and Janet were alive, they organised tea with friends. Now, we use them exclusively for the "not Valentine's Day" party. Of course, beforehand, the agency was not just about appointments with men; it was maybe more a sort of "social experiment" to find some companionship. Now, of necessity, it's something different. And although I try to maintain this ancient decor, I'm the first to realize that the situation had gotten out of hand long before now. Maybe it had also gotten out of hand for Grace and Janet, but they pretended not to notice it.

'You got a new boy.' Raymond sits before me as I get up to turn the kettle on for tea, which I keep on one of the tables beside my desk. He's not asking me, so he must have seen him enter or leave.

'Yes, he is the cousin of one of the others. He has already explained to him how it works. It was easier.'

Raymond nods and settles his glasses on his nose without replying. But he gives me one of his typical looks. Typical of when he realizes that the conversation is making me feel uncomfortable. I find it hard to be with him as I usually am with other men. As I was with that newly hired boy. I lose my stubbornness and know I must recover it as soon as possible to be credible.

'He's promising. He's young, he's clean, fresh, reassuring.'

'It looks like you're describing a new piece of furniture, Miranda.' Raymond shakes his head slightly and looks at me with his blue eyes that, despite their liveliness, always seem veiled with tears, with an indescribable sadness. Even when he's trying to be fun.

'Maybe he really is. He must please the clients; they must feel comfortable with him. I really think they'll like him.' I'm tired, and I don't feel like talking much. Not even with Raymond. I just want to sleep or leave for a long vacation and forget everything and everyone, including myself.

'And you... What do you really think?' Raymond crosses his arms and leans back in his chair. Meanwhile, the kettle has sprung, signalling the water is ready for tea. I drop two tea bags in the cups before I pour it.

'I'm not obliged to think for myself.' It's not the first time he has asked me this question, even if it has been rare for some years. 'I always choose with a view of what clients might like, not me.'

'Maybe someday you should decide to go out with someone, Miranda. Seriously, I mean.'

'No, it no longer makes sense to me now.' I concentrate even more on the tea preparation operation as if it were an extremely complicated matter and not an action that I do every day, several times a day. 'My time is over, Ray. By now, you should know how I feel.'

'Do you intend to continue this year with the usual party?' Raymond understands and changes the subject, or at least he tries.

'Of course, I'm firmly convinced. I know it started as a party against Valentine's Day created for people who feel stubbornly and proudly single. I would have avoided it sometimes, but it's a tradition introduced by Aunt Grace, and I would regret having to interrupt it.'

'Yes, maybe you're right.' Raymond smiles slightly as I hand him the cup of tea.

'I somehow have to reward myself with something true.'

No explanation is needed; Raymond knows what I mean. I hire men mainly based on their appearance. I sell a non-existent love that will never come true. I sell illusions and fake romanticism. So, I'm looking for something real for me. Definitely less charming and fairytale... but more spontaneous and, in a certain sense, even more human.

Julie

Maybe it was foolishness. Maybe it is simple curiosity. I don't even know why I got such a thing in my head. To break the routine, I think. The fact remains that, absurdly enough, I forced myself to reach the location of the dating agency that I found in the Trask appliance store, 'Secret Agents at Your Service.'

I booked an appointment online. I don't even know what I was thinking at the time. And I don't know what I'll say when I'll show up there. I passed myself off as a client, in short. But the last of my intentions is to pay to go out with a man or to be courted by "one of their boys". Getting here has already been one of the stupidest ideas I've ever had in my life.

I feel like a total idiot as I get off the bus at the Finglas Village stop, which, according to the information I found on the website, should be the closest to the listed address. I decided to just look from a distance, and then I'd run away like a good girl.

I look for the exact address with the help of Google Maps; fortunately, it exists. I find myself at the corner of a supermarket. My attention is drawn to a vagabond sitting on a low wall. She looks like a vagabond, with her clothes a little crumpled and torn. Her blue jacket has big holes in the sleeves, and you can see the orange sweater she is wearing underneath. She's very colourful, yes. She follows me with an attentive and inscrutable look just as I'm about to take a chocolate bar from my bag to restore some energy. Feeling uncomfortable, I take another bar from the package I drag from my bag and offer it to her.

'I always eat it exaggeratedly when I'm nervous or stressed...' I don't think she's interested in my eating habits; I say it just to say something. Maybe I had better keep quiet. In any case, I must find the agency and decide in the meantime if I intend to show up at the appointment or not.

'Thank you...' The woman replies just as I'm walking away. I didn't expect it; I turn towards her and meet her spontaneous but a little tired smile. 'You have a good heart. You will be lucky in love in the coming days.'

'No, I really don't think so.' I shake my head with conviction. Maybe I should have avoided answering. 'It's impossible, especially in the coming days. I bet you make the same prediction to all the women just to make them happy.'

'I'm making it to you right now.' The woman's eyes widen on me. They are of an unusual colour, a dark blue that tends towards purple. She has delicate features and thin blond hair that frames her face. It seems impossible to give her an age, although she looks like a child with too many years on her shoulders. Maybe with too much suffering and a decidedly cumbersome past.

'Hmm... thanks, anyway.' I walk away, waving at her. I have no desire or time to deepen the conversation.

Following the directions from my mobile phone, I discover that the agency's office is pretty close and it would be okay for me to walk the road right in front of me to get there.

The building that I find in front of me leaves me puzzled. It looks like a block of apartments dating back several years. I check the names and immediately see the name of the agency. Undoubtedly, I'm in the right place.

I work my courage up, and I ring the bell. It opens after a few seconds, and I hear the main door click. I go up the stairs, looking around with little conviction. Maybe it's a trap created on purpose to attract naïve girls and women a little too curious like me.

When I arrive in front of the actual door of the agency, orange and slightly peeling, I decide that I won't pull back now. I walk a few steps, and I'm welcomed by a girl who looks about my age but with much more care for clothes and makeup.

'Good morning, I'm Kara.' She introduces herself, holding out her hand. I take the opportunity to observe her raven hair that touches her shoulders and her confident attitude. Indeed, the agency really exists. Kara's behaviour is too professional; it couldn't be all a farce.

'Good morning...' I shake her hand and think again that this might be the right moment to withdraw, declaring that I made a mistake.

'You must be Juliette Bonnet, right?'

In a mellifluous voice, she confirms my identity before I can slip away. Yes, of course, I must be. I filled out the application form and the appointment form this way. My full name has a strange effect on her lips.

'Yes, it's me... Julie will do if you like.'

'Julie.' Kara repeats my name more firmly and beckons me to follow her. We walk down a corridor until we reach a door behind which I suppose there is an office.

She opens it for me, and I find myself directly in front of a woman with semi-collected brown hair on her nape and dark eyes, intense and a little sarcastic. Or it's precisely the look she directs at me that appears sarcastic, almost a challenge.

'Come in, Juliette.' The woman calls me, gesturing a little. I notice her sharp fingers moving almost impatiently.

'Julie...' I wish I hadn't written my name as it appears on my passport, but it's what I do whenever I must complete a form or something like that, in fear of making mistakes and creating confusion. But I can't make mistakes here; the only confused one seems to be me.

The woman waits for me to sit right in front of her. The desk separates us, and she keeps a slightly dated computer on her right, checking the screen at regular intervals, almost rhythmically.

'Miss Juliette Bonnet, as far as I know. I'm Miranda Crossing.' She only gives me her name as a duty; I realize this is not an actual introduction. 'The best thing to save time is to try to immediately outline the characteristics of the man you would like to meet. Do you have special requests, an ideal you would like to see materialised in real life?'

Her last words, "materialised in real life", remain particularly imprinted on me. This woman seems almost committed to making the matter the least romantic and the most mechanical possible, as if she was in a hurry to conclude and saddle me with a man as if he was a package to be bought and delivered to the addressee. Online shopping. It almost surprises me that she doesn't put pictures of her "secret agents" on the website so they can be chosen earlier without being forced to come up here. Only photos of romantic contexts are shown, but they are always taken from a distance.

'Julie, much better... and I'm not here for a man.' I express myself without hesitating, trying to communicate the concept in my best English. Miranda's accent and voice make me feel uncomfortable, almost more than her way of looking at me, which now, after my statement, becomes highly suspicious.

'Of course, I understand.' Strangely, Miranda shows unexpected discomfort. 'I realize that we are a little behind the times, and we should keep up to date, but if you're looking for a woman...'

'No, I'm not even looking for a woman. Here, I...' I don't know how to raise the question. I should just say it, and that's it. 'Actually, a woman is involved; that's me. But for a man.'

Was I clear enough? I doubt it. Miranda looks at me puzzled; I realize I am not one of her "typical clients" from how she folds her arms across her chest. She tilts her face, observing me, but remains silent, maybe waiting for me to remember the words to try to express myself better.

'I understand how important old healthy romance is to you; I mean... not that there isn't...' I sigh and bite my lips. I know where I want to get, even if it doesn't seem like that at all. 'A bit like in old movies, in short. Like... *Casablanca*...' *Casablanca*? No, what does *Casablanca* have to do with it? 'No, I mean, *Breakfast at Tiffany's*!' Here we go, maybe... she was... and he too... 'Hmm... Or *Sabrina*, always with Audrey Hepburn. Here, I would say that I could be more like Sabrina, maybe? She, too, had gone abroad to study cooking, like me. In France. But since I was already in France, more or less... Maybe I had better go to Italy and not to Ireland...'

'I understand.' Miranda nods with a smug, calm smile. 'You like the Humphrey Bogart type. Serious, reassuring, mature. He's the main actor in two of the movies you mentioned.'

'No, no...' But what did I say? I know that when I'm nervous, I mess up!

'So, you're looking for an Italian? We should have one among ours... You're French, aren't you?'

'No, not even. I'm actually Swiss, but I'm not looking for an Italian.' No, she didn't understand. Or she's making fun of me and wants me to say clearly why I'm here. 'I mean... I'm not looking for a woman, I'm not looking for Humphrey Bogart, I'm not looking for an Italian... I was wondering if there was the chance... that someone is looking for me!'

CHAPTER 8

Miranda

Obviously, I had understood for a long time what the girl was trying to suggest. I enjoyed making her suffer and letting her feel unsure of herself and her way of expressing herself.

In any case, I will have to say no. I know well that gender equality is an important thing. But I would never expose a girl to a similar risk. Not that boys can always be perfectly calm, though... All right, I might also be old-fashioned.

'So, do you take women as well to work as St. Valentine's secret agents?' The girl, Juliette or Julie, as she prefers to call herself, rummages in her bag until she finds one of our flyers. She places it under my nose and turns it in my direction.

'No, we don't hire women. Because we never had requests from men seeking women.'

'This surely happens because you have no women to offer...' she shrugs and breathes deeply. I don't know if it is more of an encouragement or a reproach. She is a pretty girl, a bit naïve. I don't understand why she came here and what or who she exactly needs.

'Often men are not content with pure romanticism... and this, in any case, is not in the spirit of the agency.' I no longer know what is and is not in the spirit of the agency, but it is better not to split hairs.

'Often not even women are content with pure romanticism.' The girl replies in kind, I must admit it.

'Yes, it would be useless to deny it.' I'm quite convinced that it was like that even earlier. But it couldn't be said, as if it was

56

forbidden to express it clearly. 'Maybe romanticism itself has long since died. Or maybe it never really existed.'

'Yet you run an agency like this...' She looks at me, confused, and she's not entirely wrong. The truth is that I don't even know why and how I ended up here. I could very well have done something else. I became accustomed to Aunt Grace, Janet, and the environment, I'm afraid.

'It just happened to me.' I inherited it, then tried to update it and keep it up with time. With poor results, unfortunately.

'The truth is that I was looking for a man at the beginning. For my friend Valerie...' She holds her breath for a moment, and then she tells me all in one go the sad story of her best friend dumped a step away from her wedding. 'I thought I would lighten up her mood a bit, as far as possible, by organising a few dates with a kind boy... sensitive... honest...'

'Yes... and maybe even handsome, intelligent, a good catch...' I add, rolling my eyes. 'Practically perfect in every way, like Mary Poppins.'

'Hmm...' she looks at me puzzled, in the end. While initially, she nodded to every adjective I used to describe this miracle man. 'I suppose you don't have anyone like that, do you?'

'No. Also, because he doesn't exist, I'm afraid.'

'Anyway... regarding the job, if I could try...' she sighs and frowns slightly. Then she relaxes and stares her blue eyes at me.

She's a pretty girl, really. She looks delicate, but she seems brave enough to come here to try something like this. And I don't feel like the usual bitch, today. Maybe I'm just a little less than normal.

'Do you really want to take a similar risk and go out with unknown clients? Without knowing what they might have in mind or what they could want from you?'

'It's the same risk I'd take going out with a "normal" guy. Who knows what men have in their heads?'

'I have to admit you're right.' She caught me off guard. But no, I won't give her the job anyway. This agency was born in a certain way and will continue working like this. As much as I can say, I make it work like this. In fact, I drag it, primarily thanks to loyal clients. I decide to completely change the subject and show myself interested in the fate of her unfortunate best friend. 'Anyway... if you still think you want to help your friend, I will have some guys available. He may not correspond exactly to all the required requisites, but he's charming and kind. Let's say he's quite new in this job, so he might be much more spontaneous than the others.'

Actually, I didn't think about offering the new employee, Michael's American cousin. I don't know how it came out, but now I might as well take advantage of the idea; he might be the right guy.

'Yes, he might be fine.' The girl still frowns slightly, then relaxes, becoming more convinced. 'Indeed, if he's a charming and nice guy...'

'I'll show you his picture, so you'll tell me if he could be the right type for your friend.'

I return to Giles McGrath's file in my crowded and messy computer. Here he is; fortunately, his file was already open. I turn the screen to Juliette and watch her reaction. Giles is cute, and he looks almost innocent. It is always better to emphasise the "almost". Nothing like his wretched scoundrel cousin with his perpetually grim expression of handsome bad boy. But of course, those who like the type will be fine with him.

'Yes, he's nice, I admit it...' she smiles and nods, pleased before frowning and slightly widening her eyes.

What's wrong with her now? I turn the screen towards myself again to check that Giles's photo hasn't turned into Freddy Krueger's photo.

'Can I think about it?' She relaxes and smiles again.

'Of course. I can show you some other guys if you prefer.'

'No, he is fine. I don't need to see others.' Leaning back in her chair, she crosses her arms. 'In the meantime, could you think about my offer? Put me to the test, at least. I could surprise you.'

Julie

I was crazy, I know. Making such an offer to that woman, offer myself, make myself available to go out with unknown men. Stating that I might even surprise her...

I know it's not like me. I know myself well enough to be aware of it. It's not in my character. I have difficulty interacting with men I have known for a while already! And then... if it is dangerous? More than it is to see someone I could meet any evening in a pub.

Yes, it's a certainty. I was crazy. After greeting her and showing self-confidence that doesn't belong to me, I leave the building and find myself in the street again. I set off quickly towards the bus stop as if I wanted to erase the traces of my passage in this area. At the corner of the supermarket, I meet the same vagabond again. The one that had made the prediction of *luck in love* for me in the coming days. I look down to ignore her. I really don't want to know about love, especially in the coming days. It would be a love born with the worst auspices; I'm well aware of that.

Crossing the city centre, I must stop by Trask Electric to collect Sarah's PC. Apparently, it is ready. I would have preferred her to go there directly. I don't like dealing with those two.

I cross the threshold and can't find anyone inside until I see the owner emerging from the back. He brings a couple of computers and gives me a smile that, despite the effort, is not very encouraging.

'Hmm... your wife told me to drop by...'

'Yes, sure. Sarah's computer... Sarah, what's her name... her friend.'

'Sarah Ward.' I help him and try not to judge him for not remembering the customers' names.

He puts the two laptops on the counter and takes refuge in the back again. Meanwhile, I see that the state of the two PCs is far from optimal. One is almost completely disassembled. The other one, which is open, shows a discouraging electric blue screen on which nothing appears. I look away to search among the advertising flyers, leaning nearby. I quickly slide them through my fingers, but not one of those of Valentine's Day is left.

Moments later, the man, Mr. Trask, returns with Sarah's computer underarm.

'Here it is. I worked on that one personally.'

His statement sounds almost like a death sentence to the poor computer. Maybe I shouldn't worry. Appearances can often be deceiving. In any case, I will carry out my personal mission. I will leave the PC at Sarah's house, and then I will go and take shelter in my house to watch a movie. Of what will follow later, I prefer not to know.

I will await Miranda Crossing's reply in the meantime. And I will make my decision. Could that guy be a good diversion for Val? Maybe. Maybe even beyond his job as a St. Valentine's secret agent.

CHAPTER 9

Giles

'Are you willing to start working straight away?'

Miranda catches me off guard as soon as I answer the phone. I had not yet entered the agency number. Only her accent allowed me to identify her immediately.

'Yes, of course.' I try to answer without hesitation, even though I'm actually starting to have a thousand doubts about it.

'Perfect! There's already a possible interested client. But first...' She pauses and sighs; it seems endless. So much so that I don't know what to expect. 'First, you'll have to be ready to pass a test. With me.'

'A test?' I repeat mechanically, even if the real question is another. With her? With Miranda? What does she mean by test? Indeed... what does she mean by a test with her?

'You see, I can't put you on the market without knowing how you're doing. That's why I must make sure of it myself.'

Put it this way, it could even seem like an indecent proposal. Not that I would mind, in fact... In my mind, I begin to fantasize. Me with Miranda. Miranda naked. Miranda above me, her lips on mine... while she whispers...

'If you were incompetent, I wouldn't want the client to complain. It would be terrible publicity.'

I become lucid and attentive again. Me, incompetent? The client? No, maybe she didn't really mean what I believe. From the beginning of our telephone conversation, I realize only now that she has used a decidedly more confidential tone with me.

'Giles... are you listening to me?'

'Yes, yes... of course!' I clear my throat and try to make a firm, confident man's tone. 'What would this test be?'

'Going out for dinner. I want to see how you behave. You must act as if I were a client, not your employer.'

Oh, here... And anyway, "employer" and "boss" certainly beat "client". Any client, any other woman, would instil less fear in me than Miranda Crossing.

'It's a test I do with everyone.' She reveals to me coldly. There is not a bit of understanding in her voice, as if she wanted to check that the machine she just bought had all the gears in the right place.

'Sure. There's no problem. I'm ready at any time.'

I even answer like a machine. Before hanging up, she tells me she would let me know the day, the time, and the place as soon as possible. I stare at the phone, still a little stunned by the attitude of this woman who strangely attracts me and upsets me at the same time. Then suddenly, a sentence of her emerges in my mind.

Speaking of me, did she really say, "Put you on the market"?

Miranda

Am I really thinking about Juliette's proposal? I know she wants to be called Julie, but she's got into my head as Juliette already, so Juliette will remain forever, whether she likes it or not.

I could test her, too; why not? I spent my whole life testing whoever happens to me. It's too bad that I'm always disappointed.

I open the files again with the boys' records. I let them pass, one after the other. Selected based on age, physical characteristics, and attitudes. I go back to Giles McGrath, the new one. The one I could assign to Juliette's friend. So no, he is not okay to test her. I want to keep him for myself; I must test him first.

Gregor, the Austrian. No, it's too mature. Antonio, the Italian. Very handsome guy with impeccable manners. He is one of the most sought-after by the ladies, but I'm afraid he has such a confident and enterprising attitude that he risks suffocating Juliette's personality. A Frenchman like Louis wouldn't be good; better to keep her from going out with one of the same nationality or the same language. It would be too easy and wouldn't often happen to her later.

I must find someone with some experience, but that doesn't scare her too much. Ron, Irish... no, too sweet. Someone who even scares her a bit is better on second thoughts! At least she will know what she must deal with and change her mind. Before she really tries to do this job elsewhere. And elsewhere, they could take advantage of her. So…

So, who's left? I go through the photographs again, one after another, repeatedly. In the end, I leave only two files open. Stephen Alden, the Australian. Or Michael Wrighton, an Irish American raised in England. Michael... or Stephen...

I close my eyes, and I lean back against the chair. It's so uncomfortable that sooner or later I'll have to decide to buy another one. Maybe I'll take a trip to the Finglas Village charity shop that deals with furniture sales; they have a lot of great deals. I have a persistent pain in my shoulders for a few days now.

I take the phone and select the number. One of the two. I'm still not entirely convinced. Michael or Stephen. I must decide without feeling personally involved because it's unfair on my part. It's inconceivable. I hope he's not busy. Or is that really what I hope for? He replies on the second ring.

'Hello. I have a job for you. Yes, it's important.'

CHAPTER 10

Giles

Any Saturday. The second day of February. It's almost embarrassing. I think February is definitely the coldest month in this country. Much worse than December and January. But this is not what is too embarrassing. The city centre is decorated with hearts of all sizes and shapes. They come out everywhere, from all the windows. Maybe I should go back to New York, where the situation will be at least ten times more embarrassing and annoying. Or perhaps I'm using the wrong word. I've never cared about Valentine's Day, not even when I was with someone. Not even in high school, when my girlfriend of the moment was pestering me for a gift, for the chocolates, with all the bullshit related to this celebration for which girls can annoy.

No, the idea of returning to New York upsets me even more. It's an unpleasant thought that doesn't abandon me whenever I give it more space than necessary.

I put my hands in my jacket pockets, and even if I don't want to, the memories take over me. I try to hold on to something else without succeeding. A story uselessly dragged on for years. Not from me. I believed in it. Or at least I was trying to believe in it. My father and his absurd convictions. Which, however, necessarily involved me too. Then my granddad... the "Irish granddad" we called him at home. And he's still proud of it.

While my father has spent years in the United States, doing everything to break away from it. Maybe he's right about this. Does it still make sense to be so tied to your roots? Feeling part of a world you had abandoned many years before to build a better life elsewhere?

My father was about three years old when his family left Ireland permanently. After leaving, my granddad's parents returned, hoping to rebuild something that had been lost for too long. Later, I believe my father came back only a couple of times to please my granddad. Then, he didn't want to know any more, creating friction in their relationship that hadn't subsided yet. His life, family, business... everything of his is American. I... I don't know what I am, who I am. By birth, I'm half American, half Irish. But I don't feel a part of anything. I'm not too American, as my father feels. I'm not too Irish, as my granddad insists on believing he is, even when he has found most of his fortune in a country he never wanted to love and recognize as his own. Because my granddad never succeeded or will ever be able to resign himself, to renounce his true country. So much so that I believe he will leave everything someday and come back himself, looking for his roots.

But in the meantime, I have landed here, however. Looking for roots that I don't care about at all. To keep a promise that was taken from me when I selected any country to take refuge in to escape the chaos of my New York life.

The truth is that I found nothing at all. Also, because I haven't done any research for now. I often repeat to myself that one day, I will do it; I will certainly do it.

My primary purpose was to get out of there physically and spiritually. Get the hell out of sight, not to see. My ex, the one I did my best for, the one who wanted to build a significant relationship. With me, while in bed, she was banged by our mutual college friend who had just set the date of his wedding with his high school girlfriend. What sordidness! It's the shame that has driven me away, the disgust. Not the broken heart. Because the truth, which I didn't dare to confess to the two traitors, is that, in part, I felt relieved. Relieved like I could never believe it. The relief you feel when you shake off the shackles of a heavy burden.

I set off beyond the Ha'penny Bridge, the ancient pedestrian bridge that crosses the Liffey and connects the two sides of Dublin, reaching the southern part of the city centre. The nickname in full, "half penny", comes from the toll that had to be paid to cross it at the time of its construction. There are others, but the Ha'penny Bridge is undoubtedly the most beautiful and characteristic.

I wander aimlessly through Temple Bar, tempted to walk into any pub. I approach and walk past Trinity College, then pick up the pace, swerving through the people wandering around Grafton Street. Finally, I cross the road to enter St Stephen's Green. A walk in the park usually helps me to relax. But it's already getting dark, and for a change, it threatens to rain from one moment to another. It doesn't matter; I still needed to get some fresh air. Frozen, indeed.

How the hell should I behave with Miranda? Now, that's not bad as a thought. At least I managed to get rid of my previous thoughts, which were too heavy and demanding. I prefer it. I'd better ask Michael directly... he was there too.

I leave the park, and I head home quickly. The good thing about this city is that knowing the secondary streets, you can get from one part to the other of the centre without transport and in a short time. Everything is at hand, and this is appreciable. I became an exceptional walker. I have always been, but I have made remarkable progress since I moved here.

I walk through Henry Street, and out of curiosity, I glance towards the Trask shop. I can see a woman arguing animatedly with Gerrit. I would like to come in to watch the scene up close, from the front row and laugh behind the back of my former boss. I'm tempted. I would do it if I could wear a cape that makes me invisible. I stop anyway. Even at a distance, it's not bad at all; I'm having too much fun. The woman seems really upset. Every

66

now and then, the assholes receive the very treatment they deserve!

Julie

I knew it. I knew there had to be something wrong. I knew he was not to be trusted. And I wouldn't care about it if I must be honest. If it wasn't for the pain in the... that I always must be involved, stuck in the middle of it, when it's not my responsibility. It's me having to deal with it as if it was my fault that this idiot tampered with and destroyed her computer!

'But it turns on...' He lights up with enthusiasm in the same way the lighting-up PC was initially illuminated by an unpromising violet-blue light that helped to increase my state of tension.

'It turns on, but all the files have been lost. And we must find them again, do you understand me? They're important, do you understand me?' I spell and continue to emphasize, "Do you understand me?" almost as if the foreigner here was him, not me. Or maybe just for this reason. I'm a foreigner, damn it. Not an idiot!

The computer turned on, but the files no longer appear in the folders or elsewhere. Actually, nothing at all can be found in any of Sarah's PC's darkest corners.

But anyway, this incompetent couldn't care less about it. If we don't recover all the files, Sarah will kill me. Not him. I will be forced to suffer her anger and her frustration. Although, in fact, she sent me here to Annette Trask's shop, which, in addition to being her friend, is also a fond reader of her blog. Annette reassured her by telling her that she had an excellent technician as an employee.

'May I talk to your wife?' Now, finally, a flash of genius. At least she'll take care of explaining the matter to Sarah. I sigh, squeezing my hands.

'My wife went to her yoga class. But I'm sure the files will be back soon; it's just a matter of patience.'

Yes, sure. They will reappear by magic. I shake my head and turn off the computer on the counter between me and Trask. I really hope that he gets on better with the other appliances he sells in the store.

I take the PC, put it in a protective case, and then fit it in my bag. I barely say goodbye, only to maintain a minimum of courtesy. It will be up to me to explain that her beloved files, much of her blog history and even some recent articles she has written are in some unknown corner of her computer's hard drive. At least, I think so. I hope she will take it out on those who deserve it, not on me!

I cross the threshold and head for home. I feel tired and confused. I don't even know if I'm following the right path. Not the one towards home. In my life, I mean. The meeting with Miranda Crossing left me a bit...

I can't finish the thought. I feel the impact of something, or instead of someone, just past the Trasks' window. My fault this time, I admit it; I must stop walking with my head down.

I recognise him instantly. It's him. But I didn't think I'd meet him again, and here of all places. The guy Miranda proposed to me for Val. Here, now, I'm even more convinced. It could be a chance meeting. And then...

'Out and about without kids? Considering how you bumped into me, I can tell who they took it from. Luckily, no little sticky hands and no flying ice cream this time.' His ironic tone annoys me, but I decide to put up with it.

'They certainly didn't take it from me because, luckily for me, I'm just the occasional babysitter.'

'Hmm... I guessed it!' He looks at me, wrinkling his nose, and then he smiles slightly. 'I was teasing you.'

'You always hang out in front of this store. Do you live nearby, or do you often have appliance problems?' I don't want to investigate him, but... okay, I'm investigating him! Not even too secretly. 'In any case, I strongly advise you against it if I can. The owner is an absolute disaster!'

'Yes, I've heard it...' he nods and takes a few steps to get away from the window after having cast a somewhat sceptical look inside. 'I think I could agree.'

We stop next to the wall. Maybe I shouldn't have a conversation with a near-complete stranger, but I'm observing and studying him well in the meantime. Because soon he may no longer be. A stranger. He looks nice, really. Tall, with a handsome face and light and thick hair. Where is he from? From his appearance, he seems Irish, but I'm never good at recognizing accents. At least his pronunciation is clear enough. He looks kind, as Miranda said. And he has those green eyes that almost seem to sparkle with an innate light when he smiles.

'They had a great technician before.' I say that just to say something. Not to look like a fool who gets lost staring at the first handsome boy she meets. Also, he still doesn't know my plans and projects, which concern him directly. 'I was told so. But he must be on vacation...'

'Yes, I confirm. They had a great technician.'

He's staring at me, too, now. What should I do? Take the chance to get to know him better, to understand who he is and how he would behave. Investigate him as much as possible; that's what I'll do!

'I'm Julie, by the way...' I decide to throw myself in and hold out my hand. I smile exaggeratedly, maybe. I'm not like that, usually. No, I'm never sociable with strangers. 'I'm going to get a cappuccino at Insomnia... if you want... if you like. I must buy the new issue of a cooking magazine, so...'

All right, now it's done! If he thanks me and refuses it, maybe it's better that...

'Yes, I'd like a cappuccino', he nods, shaking my hand. 'Nice to meet you, Julie. I'm Giles, the great technician.'

CHAPTER 11

Giles

'I left because I got a much more important and well-paid job.'

I try to look convinced and use a decisive, professional, serious tone. Then I sip the cappuccino to sink the bullshit I'm telling in caffeine. But anyway, I can't tell her that Trask kicked me out because he surprised his wife with her hand caught in the zip of my jeans.

'Of course, I understand.' Julie nods with conviction. I persuaded her! 'Much more important... and well-paid, I believe it.'

'And now you... What do you do? I mean, I already know you're a babysitter.' I shift my attention to her, which is a much better idea. In part, she really intrigues me; on the other hand, she could be helpful. I will be trained to go out with Miranda, at least. Also because I haven't been out with a woman from... okay, better not to think about it.

'Yes, I babysit those little devils only from time to time. I'm their mother's personal assistant. Sarah Ward, maybe you know her... she's a famous food blogger. I want to become one, too, so I'm trying to learn from her. The computer is hers, with all her articles and files, which I'm afraid have been completely lost. However, I'm also taking cookery classes; I attend a course where Kate Norman occasionally teaches.'

'Really interesting.' I can't understand what a food blogger is for, but it's definitely due to my limited knowledge about the subject. Shouldn't she be an actual chef? No, I can't express myself like that with her. It's certainly an important job. It's my fault; I don't understand anything about it. 'So, are you already a cooking expert? Or are you learning?'

She smiles and nods. I'm not good at showing interest in something when I really don't give a damn; I admit it. But I must exercise. Indeed, I will meet clients who I don't care about. At least she's pretty, yes.

'Yes, I'm still learning. And I'm really doing my best to become as good as Sarah. But now...' she sighs and shrugs. 'I hope she doesn't blame me for her PC. She sent me to the Trasks; it wasn't my idea. But you know how the bosses are...'

'I know; it happened to me too.' Of course, I know! But better to spare her my real misadventure with the Trasks. And anyway, I shouldn't talk about it or let it spread around; I wouldn't look good. 'But it could be an easily solved problem. The one with the PC, I mean. I can try to find the lost files if you trust me. I promise you nothing, but I can try.'

'Oh, could you really?' She smiles and stares at me. She really has beautiful blue eyes, so innocent and sweet. And the flush in her cheeks gives her an even more tender expression. 'Yes, please try it. It couldn't get much worse than it already is!'

She squeezes her hands and crosses her fingers; she looks at me as if I am the saviour of her entire existence.

'We are a little uncomfortable here...' The coffee shop table is tiny, but the truth is that I would like to get to know her better. 'We can go to my place; I don't live very far.'

'Hmm...' she seems doubtful; I'm afraid she will refuse. At this moment, she looks like Little Red Riding Hood, undecided or not on accepting the invitation of the wolf. Even if I don't really feel like a wolf, not at all. Suddenly she finishes the cappuccino left in her cup; she puts on her jacket and hat and wraps her scarf around her neck. Then she puts her bag on her shoulder. 'Yes, sure! Thank you very much, Giles. I'm sure you'll be able to recover the lost files!'

Julie

He inspires confidence in me even if I don't usually go to strangers' houses like this. Not those with whom I have spoken only once, at least. But... the fact remains that I unconsciously came across, more than once, precisely in the St. Valentine's secret agent, that Miranda has destined for Valerie. Sometimes, destiny...

So, I said to myself... Yes, well... why not try him directly? While at it, I can understand what he is like. And then maybe he'll really help me with Sarah's computer. So, I combine business... with business. Although I must admit, I don't mind his company.

He's not working, so he will be completely spontaneous with me. As he really is. At least I hope that with Val too, later, he will behave in the same way. Here, I feel like I'm spying on someone in disguise.

We arrive at his place, in his apartment on Parnell Street, after leaving the Insomnia within the Eason bookstore and having retraced part of O'Connell Street and Henry Street again. He was right; he doesn't live very far. He let me take off my jacket, hat, and scarf. While he puts them on the clothes hanger, I leave the bag on the sofa and kneel to take the computer out.

I check my mobile phone in the meantime. I find a message from Miranda. She informs me that she has decided to accept my proposal and to test me. So, without knowing it, right now, I'm just in the house of someone who could soon become a colleague of mine. It's destiny, really... I go on reading Miranda's message. Oh God, she wants to "try me" as St. Valentine's secret agent, and tomorrow night! The truth is that I didn't expect her to take me so literally. How will I do it? Will I be prepared? And above all... with whom? Maybe with an old slobbering man with octopus' hands... just to teach me a lesson and put me back in my place. Indeed, she judges me as a cocky and arrogant little French!

'Hey, are you okay?'

My future colleague returned to the living room and knelt beside me without me even noticing. Obviously, Miranda won't test me with someone like him! It would be too good and too easy! Because he is destined for clients, not for an employee in need of money.

'Yes, I'm well. Here is the PC.' I put it on the table and, standing up, I sit on the couch.

Giles sits next to me and stares into my eyes for a moment. He seems to be reflecting on something that I cannot grasp. Then he turns away from me to focus on the computer. From how he acts, he seems to know what he's doing. He's attentive and focused. On the other hand, I am not at all because all my attention is focused on him. I hardly care anymore about Sarah's files, articles, or blog.

I look at his profile, the way he slightly squints his eyes as he reflects on the problem. His hands, his fingers moving quickly on the keyboard.

'Do you think... there is any hope?' I only ask to interrupt the silence created by the fact that he's working while I'm sitting here, and I feel completely useless.

'There's almost always hope.' Giles gives me a quick look and a smile, then nods and returns to focus on work.

I also focus on Sarah's computer. I see him open one of the articles I feared had been lost. I gasp and grab his arm, holding it in my hands.

'Oh, it's fantastic!' I bite my lips, and if I followed my instinct, I'd hug him.

'I told you, there's almost always hope. The files were still there; they were just hidden.' He smiles and turns to me, winking at me.

'Thank you very much, Giles! You don't know what it means to me!' And I don't even know it myself. Maybe I don't even care so much now.

'That you won't get in trouble with your big boss, and you can get on with your work to become... a food blogger!'

'Yeah, right... food blogger.' I sigh and lean against the sofa, feeling suddenly relaxed like I haven't been in a long time. 'It may seem strange, but it's a fashionable and very profitable business.'

I don't know why I feel compelled to give explanations to him. Or maybe I'm trying to explain it to myself.

Giles turns again, this time entirely towards me. He leans with an elbow on the sofa and looks at me. The colour of his eyes is between grey and green, but some shadow shades them now.

'If that's what you want, it's fine, Julie. You don't have to explain it to others; you must be convinced.'

'Are you... convinced about your job?'

Giles is right about my idea of becoming a food blogger. But he doesn't know that I know what he does. For what job he left his work with the Trasks.

'No, not at all, if I must be honest. Julie, sometimes you are forced to adapt to the circumstances, hoping to do the right thing.'

'Yes, Giles... I understand what you mean. More than you can imagine.'

CHAPTER 12

Michael

And so, Giles got the job from Miranda. I'm sure she wouldn't even consider him if it wasn't for me. Giles is certainly not her type. Not that anyone in there is. Not necessarily.

At least we have agreed that she won't replace me, the bitch. With the excuse of my flu. Which never even existed. She invented it to create problems for me. She has changed in recent years. More and more. And she does nothing but get worse. And I know the reasons. The reason, indeed. She keeps it tightly closed in her desk drawer. And I realise that it has nothing to do with me.

Sometimes, she acts so automatically that she makes me think she's becoming a machine: diabolical, cold, cynical. No, a machine doesn't conjure up the right image. Hateful, moody, and perpetually angry. She has been like that since the beginning, though.

I'm still on my way. I'm walking O'Connell Street back and forth like an idiot. I call from here because I don't want Giles to hear me and start asking me more questions in case he's at home. I have decided now. I will leave anyway. But on my own initiative, not because she will kick me out.

He doesn't answer, I leave him a message. He already knows what I need anyway; we've talked about it a lot lately, even though I've never taken him seriously.

'Hi, Stephen. Send me the exact address to access the site; I've decided to register this evening.'

Never in my life would I have thought and much less hoped of becoming a cam boy. Anyway, I would never have dreamed of becoming a chaperone to lonely ladies and being part of Miranda's agency as St. Valentine's secret agent or any other celebration, occasion, or anniversary to satisfy any desire clients express towards me. And Miranda deceives herself... obviously, she deceives herself that her illustrious and wealthy clients don't want sex. They want it, all right, almost always. And even if it's not in the agreements, in the contract that they signed and that I signed myself as an agency employee, they always try, even at the cost of paying something more to the person concerned.

But she pretends not to know, not to understand. Miranda Crossing. Will she have realised that, unlike others, I haven't reached that point? Probably not. Because she doesn't care.

In any case, it's better to work in front of a camera than for her. She won't like it and will kick me out if she learns of it. As she will also kick Stephen out, who has decided to leave anyway. I'll sell my body to unknown clients watching me behind a screen, protected from a distance that cannot be filled. Always better than selling my soul to her. I've been working a long time now for Miranda Crossing; I have become even more obvious and superfluous than the furnishing of her office, which for years she has decided not to change due to a senseless attachment to the past.

She won't like losing both me and Stephen. We've been with her for years. We even prepared the flyers for her advertising campaigns and developed a marketing strategy with her. When Miranda didn't even know where to start; she has a degree in ancient history. What the hell does she do with ancient history if she sells chaperones for ladies for a living? She even completed a PhD here in Dublin just as she started managing the business with her aunt.

I was nineteen when I entered, after meeting Stephen, and it was just a game for me, a diversion to round off my earnings, and less stressful than my job as a department store salesman. I can't believe more than ten years have passed. Miranda had just arrived from England with her arrogance, impeccable accent, and the idea of becoming a great professional after her doctorate, the most outstanding expert on ancient history. She was still married at the time. Then he ended up in that drawer, where he never left. And he didn't even leave her head.

I finally return home. I'm nervous, and I keep coughing. Miranda is right about this; I won't be able to work under these conditions. Already from the door, I hear voices coming from the living room. The distinguishable voice of Giles and that of a girl.

Arriving in the living room, I see them sitting on the couch with a computer before them. I think they might be watching a movie or a video, but he's explaining to her something about certain files. I glance from behind and notice the image of a kind of vegetable soup. Did Giles invite a woman home to talk about cooking?

'Hey, hi!' I raise my hand greeting, ready to retire to my room.

'Hi...' Giles looks embarrassed, and I don't understand why. 'Julie, he's my cousin Michael.'

The girl, Julie, gets up from the couch to shake my hand. Fine, now I'm really going to withdraw. However, I wonder if Giles plans to do something with the girl.

'Hi, Giles fixed my computer.'

'Oh, right...' The embarrassment is obvious. Likely, she's here just for that.

'I advise you to take some honey with a bit of lemon. For your cough, I mean.' Julie smiles, and I take a moment to understand that she's talking to me. 'It worked with me. The Irish weather almost destroyed me during the fall.'

'Tell me about it; it always destroys me! For over a decade.'
I say so much just to say something, and then I force a smile and
wave again.

They both nod, Giles and Julie. I leave without trying again
to make conversation. It's not the girl's fault, of course. She's
pretty and probably very nice. But I'm so out of my mind lately.

I hope, however, that she won't stay long. She doesn't seem
too intimate with Giles. She really seems to be here just to fix
her computer.

Because tonight I want to try my first webcam video, I'm just
waiting for Stephen to reply by telling me the site address. And
I prefer not to have strangers around.

Giles

Julie left with her computer. I gave her my phone number in case
she has other problems. I'm confident she won't. It was just an
excuse to try to keep in touch with her.

As soon as Julie left, Michael returned to the living room, and
now he looks at me quizzically.

'All done? Was she really here just to get her PC repaired?'

'She had lost some files; we found them. All done.'

Michael crosses his arms over his chest; he doesn't seem
entirely convinced. He rather seems to want to add something;
he's silent instead. I take this chance to tell him about the matter
with Miranda. And ask him for some advice since he knows her
so well.

'Miranda wants to test me...' I snort, putting my arms behind
my head. 'Should I prepare myself? I don't know how. What I
mean... What should I expect from her? I must go out with her;
honestly, that woman makes me nervous.'

'Oh, you're not interested in the girl who just left?'

Michael stares at me. Now, he looks pissed for some reason that escapes my understanding. And I don't even understand what his question has to do with what I asked him about Miranda and the test she'll submit to me.

'No, I mean... I don't know, I didn't think about it.' I thought about it but don't want to go too far now. I don't see the reason, and I have other things on my mind anyway. 'Why? Are you interested in her?'

'What the fuck do I know... I hardly saw her! I don't even remember her face anymore, what she looks like!'

All right, I give up. He's really pissed off; he doesn't just look like it. I don't know what went wrong with him today. I don't even ask because I know that when he acts like that, he's certainly not going to tell me about it. However, it has been going on for a while.

He leaves without another word. And without answering and helping me with my next meeting with Miranda. All right, I understand. I'll have to deal with it alone. I'm not a beginner, anyway. I had several girls. So, I won't let myself be intimidated by a woman, even if she has an icy and austere look. Even if she's sensual, provocative and will do anything to embarrass me. Even if she'll become my boss. Even if she is Miranda Crossing.

CHAPTER 13

Julie

I can get to Sarah's house before she returns. Giles saved my life, literally. I had time to check, and everything seemed to be there. I realize that it wasn't my fault. But anyway, I felt responsible. Maybe because I'm the first to suffer every daily annoyance in Sarah's life, her bad mood directly affects my work and my future career hopes.

As soon as she returns, I explain what happened to her quickly. She seems to show little attention. Nor does she care how much I did to get her back her beloved computer and my care that all the files were saved. She's only interested in having it back in perfect condition.

'Very well, I'm going to update my blog immediately. I have already written the notes for my next article. My readers are waiting for me and anxious without any news from me! This is the evening dedicated to questions and answers online...' she smiles, showing exaggerated enthusiasm. She moves her head, letting her blond hair swing over her shoulders. 'The children are about to return with their nanny, Susan, but she can't stay. Can you keep them quiet for just an hour? Charles is about to return.'

The translation of 'just an hour' in Sarah's language means the whole goddamn evening. Part of me regrets not having returned her the computer as it was when I went to pick it up from the Trasks. Because I know well that Charles, her husband, will completely ignore me and his children to go and hide in his office under the guise of an urgent business. 'After all, my wife will have almost finished.' Yes, of course. You bet!

'All right, but I must go to class in an hour. Otherwise, I'll be late, and you know I can't with Kate.' No way, my dear Sarah. This time, I won't let you push me around or let your beloved businessman husband ignore me.

'Okay...' she sighs, shrugging her shoulders almost casually.

As never before, I realise it's an "Okay" of sufficiency, said by someone who doesn't really care about my priorities and problems. Because only her own matter, this is the sad and disappointing truth!

So, I act accordingly. Fortunately for me, the children are tired from the day spent in school, their various activities, and the park. For once, they sit quietly in front of the TV, miraculously without arguing about which program to watch.

I begin to prepare myself for the escape. I won't give Charles the time to fight back and understand the situation. When I hear his car pass the gate, I wear my jacket, scarf, and hat. I greet the children, who give me a distracted and almost annoyed look, and I await the man at the door. So that while he comes in, I'm ready to go out.

'Good evening, Charles. The children are quiet in the living room. Sarah is busy with her blog and her readers. I must go, goodbye.'

'Oh, yes... that's fine. No, wait... wait, Julie, I should...'

I turn and smile; I pretend not to understand. Sometimes, pretending to be a dumb foreigner unfamiliar with English is incredibly useful. I've already bolted out. Running towards the headquarters of the cooking school, which fortunately is not too far from Sarah's house, near the Smock Alley Theatre. Or I'm the one who has now taken the habit of running anywhere in this town. After all, in the city centre, almost everything is within walking distance.

Kate's courses are expensive. Too expensive for my pockets. In fact, after this, in which she intervenes only once a week and I've been forced to pay in instalments, I don't think I can afford another, at least for a while. But after all, professionalism is paid for. And Kate's vegetable course is one of the most famous and essential. A basic course. Then there are the others, obviously. I'll think about it.

Sarah certainly doesn't pay me enough. Even with some translation from English into French, I don't earn enough. But maybe with Miranda, I could do it. And going out for lunch and dinner doesn't seem so demanding to me. I know, it's the kind of job that could get me in trouble. And that I can't reveal it to anyone, ever. Not even to Valerie. Unless they discover me out at dinner with wealthy and unknown men, taking me for a fully-fledged escort. But Miranda doesn't seem to me the type that would oblige me to go out with just anyone. Hers will be a select clientele; at least, I hope so. I could try, though. Giles also works for her. So maybe I should really trust her. I don't have many alternatives; if I looked for a "normal" job, I would have much less time to try to make my dream come true. I've decided now. I can only trust her.

Miranda

I wish something would happen. I can't even say what, exactly. Anything that would take me out of this uncomfortable, annoying situation.

Meanwhile, leaving the office, the only sensible thing I can do is walk home. I just need to cross the street for this. Sometimes, I would like to live farther away to have time to think and reflect while walking. I realize I could go for a walk, but I don't feel like it. Walking without a precise destination around the centre of Finglas Village and then turning back is not very exciting. I occasionally go to the area's pubs just to keep Raymond company.

'Love will soon come on your way...'

Here she is, inevitable. The usual Tally, at the corner of the supermarket. She recognises me even from a distance now. Even when I don't go to the supermarket to do my shopping. I give her an impatient look. She returns with a toothless but sincere smile. Tally and her inevitable prophecies. Tally, who believes in fairy tales. Tally, who maybe still waits for love. Even there, sitting on the ground or "perched" on the wall. Undaunted, she waits. She has a confident and obstinate look behind her fragile, almost immature appearance. All trust and obstinacy I have lost and let go a long time ago. Everyone knows her by now, Tally. Few are informed about the details of her true story. I never wanted to know it, really. Some call her "the angel of Finglas Village", maybe because she always has a good word for anyone who walks by.

'Sure, Tally. I don't doubt it.' Now, I answer her only out of habit, without considering her. 'Love is always on my path... but for others.'

She absorbs my words seriously, and then she bursts out laughing.

'Someone gave me chocolate. This is love, too. Something sweet.'

'Are you complaining that I never offer you something sweet but just money, Tally?' I stop on her side of the street, the same side of my house. I look at her, a little annoyed. Even the old, dear Tally is starting to complain and protest against me; this is unbecoming. 'At least with the money, you can buy yourself something healthier. Whoever offers you chocolate doesn't do you any good; sweets ruin the few teeth you have left.'

Not that there's much left to ruin by now. But the principle doesn't change. Tally doesn't get upset. Not anymore, not with me. She continues to laugh, almost as if I had just complimented

84

her. She's always like this, regardless of who passes by, who shows interest in her presence or who ignores her completely.

Of course, the principle doesn't change. Gifts are useless. A useless waste of time and money. I grew up like that, without gifts. My mother wasn't like Aunt Grace. She was a cold and unfriendly woman; maybe I took more from her than I had hoped and wanted. Then I got a gift. Or at least I thought I got it. Love on my way, as Tally says. But it left as it arrived. Because love doesn't even exist. Nor does romance, but no one dares to say it. Me neither. Indeed, I would dare to say it, but I can't because it would mean that my business is based on nothing, on something that doesn't exist.

CHAPTER 14

Julie

It's early morning, and I don't have to go to Sarah. But I get up anyway. I spent a night agitated by strange and rambling dreams. Kate's course went very well; it was fascinating. The problem is me. I'm starting to question so many things lately. Maybe it's just stress and tiredness. But I don't feel sure of anything anymore.

Or it could be the tension of knowing what awaits me tonight. I will have to meet my "selector". The one who will test me on behalf of Miranda, in short. And I don't feel at all calm and peaceful. I don't think he's a casual client. I'm pretty sure he's one of Miranda's right-hand men. I'm still waiting for her message to know exactly when and where I will have to meet him.

I throw back the blankets with a kick. If I give in to sleep again, I will never be able to wake up! I'm not convinced at all, but I won't back down now. After all, the idea was mine. And even though I realise it was the stupidest idea I've ever had in life, it's done now. I can try, at least.

I wrap the blanket around me, the one I keep on the chair near the wall, and I head for the kitchen. Soon, Valerie will get up to go to work. I'll make breakfast for her, too. I'm trying to be a good friend, to make life easier for her. But I can't always do it. The truth is that I don't want her to leave because I wouldn't know what to do here alone.

'Hi...' Valerie walks into the kitchen sleepily but smiles at me. 'You always manage to get up before me.'

'Not always.' I shrug my shoulders as I pour the water into the teacups.

Valerie nods and takes the muffins from the shelf.

'Anyway... I'm still thinking about it. I'm not entirely sure I'll leave.' I wonder why she wants to talk about it this early in the morning. She sits down and nibbles a chocolate muffin while I hand her a cup of tea.

'Hmm...' I wait until the toast is ready, and I take the jar of Nutella and the one of peanut butter. 'I realised I'm no longer sure of anything, Val.'

'Since when? I thought you were convinced you wanted a job like Sarah's. You're studying to become like her, aren't you?'

'Yeah, but maybe that kind of job doesn't want me.'

'You're a little weird, Julie. Did something happen?' She scans me carefully, just as if she was reading my face. As if it is visible that I'm about to start a career as a chaperone for men.

'No...' Now I feel more than ever that I've got it all wrong. I shouldn't have. It was just a challenge. It was the meeting with Miranda that pushed me towards this absurd proposal.

'It seems so to me. Are you sure nothing really happened? Have you met someone?' Valerie doesn't give up, and my lack of conviction in denying it makes her even more suspicious.

'No, I told you. Really...' Maybe I should introduce the discourse about the agency. But I can't. No, it wouldn't be a good idea for Val at all. Not if she knew it, at least. Everything should happen spontaneously, naturally, as it should do. I try to muddy the waters with a joke. 'You know, I wouldn't even think about meeting anyone now. It's a bad time for me! I would avoid it at all costs.'

What if Valerie ends up falling in love with Giles? It would be a disaster because he's paid to go out with women and be kind. So, I think it's much better to stop everything with Miranda, at least for Val and Giles. Because Giles is... yes, undoubtedly Valerie could fall in love with him. If the boy

87

offered by Miranda is really Giles, he could be the type for which a girl in Valerie's situation would lose her mind. So, instead of helping her recover from Trent's abandonment, I would end up causing her even more damage.

A diversion is good and can facilitate recovery. But falling in love, not!

'Julie, can you tell me what you're thinking about?' Valerie waves her hand before me, trying to divert me from my thoughts.

I was disconnected without even realising it.

'Nothing. Maybe I'm still sleepy, I've had strange dreams and...' I shake my head, trying to get rid of the absurd thoughts and even more absurd intentions of the last days. 'I'm thinking about work. How can I become a good chef and a food blogger like Sarah? But I'm starting to fear I don't have the right requirements.'

'I don't think so; you're good!' Valerie smiles and nods with conviction. I know, deep inside, that she is saying it only to comfort me and, above all, because she is my friend. She doesn't really believe it. Besides, I am no longer sure I really believe it. 'I'm thinking of teaching French to foreigners, as I did in France. I don't know if I will succeed; it's just an idea for the moment. Here, the truth is... I know this job could make me think of Trent because that's how we met. As soon as I arrived here, I accepted the first job I came across, just to do something and not stay home waiting for his return in the evening. But the connection between teaching and my ex doesn't hurt me that much anymore. I should have tried it before, and this was my intention after... after the wedding and honeymoon, even though Trent wanted me to work with him in his family's company. I don't know what I could have done since they produce hydraulic systems, but...'

She tries to be convincing, but I still have some doubts. Things between Valerie and Trent have only finished recently. Too short. 'Val, it hasn't been long since it ended, don't pretend with me.'

'Julie... Julie, you don't understand. I suffered, yes. But the truth is that I...' she sighs and shakes her head. 'I was upset because he was the one who wanted to end our relationship. Because I thought I'd move here, have a different life. I didn't even care how. Different. With someone to take care of me. Not necessarily Trent. It was already over, even before he left me, even before he betrayed me. I already suspected it but didn't want to see the signs. Above all, it was already over because I had tried to believe it... but I wasn't in love with him. I've never been.'

Giles

I have no desire at all, and I'm not in the mood. But tonight, I will have to go out with Miranda. Now that I think of it clearly, it seems crazy to me. What the hell came into my mind?

I must prepare psychologically for the assaults of that woman. I already know that she will attack me in every possible way, trying to embarrass me. And she will enjoy doing it. I tried to share my concerns with Michael, but the only response I received from him was indifference. And a shrug. Indifference, precisely.

'So, are you really convinced?'

Towards evening, when I'm almost ready to leave and go to the appointment, he "wakes up" from his lethargy. From his question and sceptical look, I realise he hasn't forgotten about my evening with Miranda.

'And you are convinced about putting your acrobatics on a site while you undress? And becoming a... what the hell is it called...'

My answer wasn't very friendly, but he really deserved it. Because he has been an asshole lately. He could help me, give me some tips to deal with Miranda, he knows her well! Instead, he has been an asshole, in fact. The one who doesn't give a fuck. And he's perfectly good at it, I must say.

'For that matter, I've already become one since last night. I enjoyed myself. And I'm starting to make money.'

He gives me a sarcastic and deliberately pleased look. He scans me from head to toe like I was a laboratory specimen to be analysed. It might be how I dressed. But I know him quite well. So much so that he looks at me more unhappily, more pissed and surlier than ever. But I could be wrong.

'Well... if you're happy...' After all, I still hope he helps me with some suggestions. Instead, he turns his back, walking to his room. I still try to make myself heard. 'Anyway, I'm going out. Should I say hi to Miranda from you?'

I do it on purpose. I intentionally instigate him. He was the one who suggested me for this job; why is he upset now? But maybe it isn't necessarily my fault. Who knows what's on his mind these days?

I feel like an idiot. Maybe I dressed up too much, but I can already imagine that woman's disgusted expression if I showed up in jeans and a sweater. Perhaps even casual isn't enough for her. Unless she wants to make a fool of me. And I'm sure Miranda is the kind of woman happy to make a fool of anyone, including me. Maybe my blue suit, the only one I have in the closet, is excessive, now that I think about it. I'm trying to remember how Michael usually goes out. I've never seen him in a suit, but I'm not entirely sure. Maybe he changes elsewhere. If only the asshole were in the mood to help me!

I meet Miranda in an Italian restaurant in Bray, quite well-known in the area and very popular. So, I was forced to take the DART to get there. Why go all this way? Wasn't the centre of Dublin chic enough for her? What does she want, then? The romantic walk on the seaside in this cold? She's capable of it, I bet!

As soon as I see her appearing, all my worst suspicions become a reality. Here, I imagined it. She wears dark jeans and a light blue embroidered sweater under her jacket. Her hair is loose on her shoulders, and she is almost completely without makeup. She smiles, tilting her head as soon as she sees me. She was more elegant in her office. I imagined that she would take the piss out of me!

'You look very well.' She looks at me and examines me like Michael did a little while ago. She also has the same sarcastic expression in her eyes!

'Thank you, Miranda. I also think...' I feel I'm blushing. What am I saying?

She gives me an amused look, slightly turning towards me as if she intended to embarrass me. And she succeeds well despite being silent.

'I'm glad you think, Giles.' She indicates a table after the waitress escorted us to our place.

Oh, yes... I should move the chair to allow her to sit! I swear, I usually never get so clumsy. Never!

I move to precede her, and Miranda sits down. I stand a moment behind her, trying not to indulge in the instinct to strangle her.

Surprisingly, I resist, and after a deep breath, I sit before her. I fear the worst is yet to come. We haven't ordered, and, theoretically, we should also have a conversation where I can show her my manly charm and make her feel like the most desired woman in the place. A mission impossible, in short. Especially if I have the distinct impression that the woman in question is waiting for nothing more than to embarrass me and then laugh at me!

Suddenly and unexpectedly, she rests her elbows on the table, stretches towards me and smiles.

'Don't be so tense. You're doing fine.'

Her dark eyes in mine give me an unexpected thrill. The truth, which I dare not to admit, is that I have the distinct feeling that the very opposite of what should be happening is happening. It seems that Miranda is seducing me, not vice versa. In short, I could be the hypothetical client, not her.

'It's not true...' I sigh and pull back, leaning my back against the chair. I can't take it anymore; at this point, it's better to be clear and stop her from making fun of me. 'Miranda, I know I'm not suitable. I understand it myself. No need to make me feel like an idiot. In short, can we simply eat something without obligation? Or if you have better things to do...'

'You don't want to work for me anymore?' She braids her fingers and frowns; now, she looks almost disappointed rather than contemptuous or annoyed.

'No, that's not the point. I just... well, I'm not Michael. And I'm not even Stephen. Okay, I don't know the others, but...'

'I don't think I asked you to be Michael or Stephen.' She rolls her eyes and sighs. 'Not all women like types like Michael, Stephen, or other guys at the agency. Could you please do me the favour of being yourself to the best of your ability, Giles? Without trying to imitate someone else or interpret what I'm thinking about you? Because one of the things that really annoys women, all women, is the lack of spontaneity in a man.'

'I'm sorry.' I look down. Now, I really feel like an idiot. The former one was only a pale imitation.

'I'm afraid you're not suitable for the job, Giles. You're too good a guy to fake an interest you don't feel. But I would still like to give you a chance.'

As I guessed! "Good guy" corresponds to incapable or inept. That is precisely what women say when they want to get rid of someone. A variation of "I consider you my best friend." Then they all actually run after those like Michael and Stephen.

'All right, I understand. And no, don't give me a chance. I prefer not to inspire compassion. What do you want to eat?'

I grab the menu as a defensive weapon against her and her false condescension towards me.

'Well, when you act all hurt, at least you bring out a bit of character!' She laughs out loud, and she looks at the menu too. 'I'll have the house cheese pizza.'

'Oh, damn it, Miranda. Did I dress like a penguin to come and eat pizza?' I lower the menu and look at her. She seems less cynical. Sweeter and decidedly younger.

'It was your choice.' She nods and continues to smile.

'I wanted to make a good impression...' I sigh and close the menu, moving it to a corner. 'What the hell, pizza for me too!'

'Well, now that you're a little relaxed... try to make the evening pleasant and interesting for me, new St. Valentine's secret agent.'

CHAPTER 15

Julie

I can't get Valerie's words off my mind. Wasn't she in love with Trent? What does she mean she wasn't in love with Trent? This would mean that I didn't understand anything about my best friend! Okay, maybe I'm not the one who misunderstood everything... well, if she wasn't in love with him, it was still a great imitation!

Now, however, I must temporarily set the matter aside to meet the man proposed by Miranda. She sent me his photograph on my cell phone. A great-looking guy, no doubt about it. With a determined look and very, very confident.

We have an appointment to meet at an Irish restaurant on O'Connell Street, on the corner of North Earl Street. I approach and look at James Joyce's statue so as not to give the impression I am looking for someone in an overly anxious way. To avoid mistakes, I wore a dress in light shades under an emerald green coat... or maybe it's Irish green.

I notice him out of the corner of my eye. I recognise him; he's already there. I then move my attention more clearly from James Joyce to him. And I really pretend to recognise him now. I make a surprised expression, and then I hasten to apologize for my delay even though I'm perfectly on time.

'It's me that was early, don't worry!' He smiles and slightly wrinkles his nose in an almost bold grimace. That looks bold on *his* face, at least.

He's the classic type who would make a girl like me drop to the floor at a glance. However, I stand up perfectly, thankfully.

'Anyway, I'm Julie...' I introduce myself in case he hasn't been informed.

'Juliette, I was told.' He nods, smiles, and shakes my hand. 'I'm Stephen.'

He has a hoarse and provocative voice, a man who has lived a bit. And the appearance of one who has gone through so many, being around the block, some would say. Did Miranda do it on purpose to mess my head up? I bet she did! But she won't succeed!

'I prefer Julie,' I repeat with conviction as he gently caresses my back, inviting me to follow him into the restaurant.

'Julie is fine too. They suit you both.'

He's wearing a leather jacket over a blue shirt and black trousers. He's drop-dead sexy; most looks are on us when we get in. Not just the female. His blue eyes run through the room, and then he rubs his hand over his chin.

'Miranda told me she booked under my name.'

He asks for information from one of the boys at the door, who takes us to our table. Now that we face each other, I can see him even better. I decide to immediately come out swinging so as not to let myself be intimidated by his ostentatious charm.

'How long have you been working for Miranda?'

'For too long, I'm afraid,' he sighs and rolls his eyes. 'And you... Why would you want to work for her?'

Well, he quickly dismissed my question and focused on me.

'Because I need to. And because...'

Because I was an idiot! I avoid saying it, but I think so with all my heart.

'I'm sure a beautiful girl like you won't have any problem.' He stares into my eyes. As if he wanted to undress me and, at the same time, turn me over on the restaurant table. He is the one creating problems for me right now!

He also stretches a hand to touch mine, rubbing my back with his thumb.

'But I...' I blush and don't know how to react. He really caught me off guard.

'Rule number one, Julie. Hold the overly pushy clients off. You should do it firmly but without offending them. And without blushing, my dear.'

He breaks away from me and pulls back, leaning on the couch. It was a test, then! It was all a damn test!

'Oh, damn it! You pulled one over on me...'

'It's a good thing, so next time you won't be fooled by others. At least I'm not a client.'

I'm about to reply that I strongly doubt that clients are as attractive and provocative as he is, but I hold back. I smile instead, trying to show how calm I can be, always within the limits of my possibilities.

'Yeah, better this way...' I sigh and look at him, trying to display a strength of character and confidence. 'Anyway, I think it's different for you men.'

'It certainly is, but we also have our difficulties.' He shrugs his shoulders and runs his hand through his short hair. 'Tell me a little about yourself, Julie. What are you doing here in Dublin? Where do you come from exactly?'

'I'm here to study cooking...' I'm no longer convinced, but keeping the official version is better. 'I'd like to become a food blogger. I come from Geneva.'

'Oh really? My mother has French origins, and I would like to resume it. As a child, she always spoke to me in her language; I understood it well.'

'And your mother is now...' I'd like to ask him if she knows what he's doing in Dublin, but I hold back.

'She's in Sidney.' Fortunately, he precedes me. 'I was born in Australia. I haven't been home for so long.'

'I've never been there.'

We keep talking about this and that. He doesn't embarrass me anymore; I'm getting used to him. He talks about his childhood in Australia and his marketing and design studies. I tell him something about me while we taste some typical dishes of Irish cuisine. I let him advise me; he knows the place better than me.

Almost at the end of our evening, I can't stop myself.

'What will you tell Miranda?' I know I shouldn't have asked that directly, but I don't care now.

'I'll tell her...'

'No, wait!' I suddenly change my mind and raise a hand to stop him. 'I don't care to know.'

'Are you interested in someone?' He returns to look me in the eyes with the provocative expression he had before dining. 'It has nothing to do with your earlier question about Miranda...'

'I had guessed that.' I smile and shrug my shoulders. He doesn't fool me anymore with that seducing look. 'Anyway, there might be a guy... I just met him, but the situation is a bit complicated. And for you? Is there anyone?'

'For the moment, there's only work. I have no alternative.'

He doesn't specify why he has no alternative, and I don't investigate further. He pays the bill, and we leave the place. He offers to walk me home, and I accept. We walk mainly in silence, mixing among the other people who wander through the city centre. We're two foreigners away from home. We're two souls who have met for an organized appointment and may never cross destinies again.

We pass one of the bridges separating the city's north and south sides across the River Liffey. I lose myself for a moment, watching it flow under the bridges as if it were a kind of lifeblood running through the city's beating heart. In front of my house, Stephen bids farewell with a quick kiss on my cheek, turns and leaves. He returned to being a stranger to me. I enjoyed spending the evening with him, even as a test, but so it must be and will be.

And I don't care if I've passed this bloody test. I don't care what he will tell Miranda about me. I don't even care if he was kind and easy-going to me while he actually thinks I'm a fool who feels embarrassed for a compliment that isn't even very sincere.

I know that I must and will have to endure everything. Even this strange work if Miranda decides to take me with her. I just have to set aside some money for the courses. Then, I will finally become a famous and renowned food blogger. And this sad and miserable life will end, once and for all. I will no longer be an unknown, ordinary girl who happened to be in Dublin by chance.

'Did you go out with someone?' As soon as I enter the house, Valerie's question catches me off guard. Also, she looks like someone who already knows the answer perfectly well.

'Yes, but nothing special. It was just a business meeting.' I wouldn't want to go into the conversation with her. Otherwise, I would have to tell her all the rest of it.

'Look, I saw him from the window. With someone like that, I think there's very little work involved!' Valerie laughs with amusement and winks at me.

She misunderstood everything, but I can't tell her that for Stephen, I was just a test, an employee to be subjected to a selection.

'I assure you it was just work. He is... a real food connoisseur. A consultant, in short.' Yes, that's it. I haven't even strayed too far from the truth.

Besides, I feel like food to offer to clients. And Stephen just selected me. But in the end, he's food too. And Giles is also. Maybe, more or less, we're all food that someone will examine and select to judge whether it is edible or not. And I realize, only now, that it's all very sad. But it works like this. And in some way, sometimes unfortunately, a sneaky and mean way, it will continue to work like this.

Michael

I know she did it on purpose. I didn't tell him so as not to make him suspicious. Or not to let him imagine that he's more important than he really is.

She did it on purpose; maybe she's having a good time in bed with him right now. Giles, after all, is easy to get for someone like her!

I won't let her go smoothly this time. I'll leave her to her fate, I've decided. Just like Stephen, even though she doesn't know it yet.

Now the show begins. And not just the one I intend to offer in front of the webcam. I take off my shirt and throw it on the bed. Then I wear it again, better keep it at the beginning. I must look for the right music, I select it from my computer. And I don't find anything that stimulates me enough, damn it. I just feel I'm going crazy. I should try to copy Stephen; for him, it seems so easy!

No way, what the fuck am I doing! I walk away from the screen and throw myself on the bed. What will there ever be to look at? I'm not focused. I must stop thinking. I'll blow everything up right now.

I'm not even sure about what I really want to get. I want to let her go, yes. But how? She's always there, like an obsession in my mind. An obsession that I can't uproot or tear away.

I try again; I must succeed! Maybe thinking just about her could be helpful in some way. Well, yes. In the end, she could really help me with something.

I can't avoid her. Her hands caressing me, her lips on me, her moans, her breaths... her way of whispering my name...

And in the end, I don't care if she slept just with my cousin! With how many others has she done it? She'll throw them all away anyway, like she did with me. Because the only one that remains constant is the one closed in her desk drawer. The others are just a diversion, an alternative to boredom. As for me, are the other women, after all. Better disappear. Maybe I should move elsewhere as soon as possible.

I close my eyes. Nothing will come of it tonight. I'll start tomorrow. I lied to Giles; I haven't managed to do anything yet. I cover my eyes with one arm and have the light off, but the glare penetrating through the window bothers me. And also the noise coming from the street.

Then I perceive another, closer. The key that turns in the entrance lock. So, he's back.

I know I should keep to myself and stay in my room. Pretend to sleep, not care, or mind my own business. But no, I can't resist. I jump out of bed, and in an instant, I'm in the living room before he retires to his room, and I can't pretend anymore that our meeting is casual.

I head towards the fridge, almost ignoring his presence. I'm not even thirsty, but I'll get a beer anyway.

'Oh, hi...' I give him a careless look, yawning loudly. 'Already back?'

'Yes, already back. And do you want to stop treating me like a jerk?'

I look at him, puzzled; I even forget my beer.

'What the fuck...'

'No, I'm the one who should say what the fuck!' Giles stares at me; seeing him so furious doesn't often happen.

I don't understand what he's saying and why. Unless... no, I don't think so. I sigh, and I don't reply; I wait.

'Specifically... what happened between you and Miranda? I had understood that even before, anyway.'

'Nothing worth telling.' I run my hand through my hair and hold it over my head. I'm nearly halfway between the fridge and the living room exit. I'm tempted to leave without taking anything to slip away from the situation as quickly as possible.

And without giving explanations, above all. Because there really aren't any.

'You're mad at me because I went out with her. But if this is what worries you, I can tell you that for me, it was absolutely no pleasure to see that woman, indeed!' He challenges me with an arrogant look that he doesn't often assume. 'It was a task that I would have gladly avoided.'

'Forget it; there's no need.' I decide to forget that I was thirsty; I walk past him to go and take refuge and vent my anger in my bedroom.

'She doesn't do it with everyone, does she? That of going out publicly. Not even with you.' He doesn't give up; he persists with a sadistic smile. 'But I think she treats all of you like pieces of meat to take to bed? You were right; she's a bitch. And she's also a...'

No, that's enough! He exaggerated! And how does he dare?

I turn abruptly, and in an instant, I'm on him, grabbing him by the collar of that stupid elegant blue jacket he's still wearing.

'One more word about her and I...'

'But isn't it the same as you always say?'

He takes me off guard once again. I let him go for a moment, trying to recompose myself, to reflect.

'I've never talked about her like that! And then I... I...' I sigh and pull away from him; I step back and lower my head. 'I can.'

'You can because you don't really think it. Is that what you mean?'

I really withdraw this time. Without replying. Without attacking him. Without reacting to the provocation that Giles managed very cleverly to implement against me. I fell into his trap like an idiot.

But he was right about one thing. Miranda never goes out with the agency's boys publicly. Never. She has never done it. Not even with Stephen, whom she has known for years. Not even with me. If she must test them, she lets them out with loyal clients.

Does she treat us like pieces of meat to take to bed? Probably. I fooled myself, thinking I was the only one. To be the only one. Because I wanted her. And my main problem, now, is that I still want her.

CHAPTER 16

Giles

I was an asshole; I realize it. But at least now, it's clear how things really are. I had already suspected it for a while, even before Michael arranged a job interview for me with Miranda.

Maybe I should really let it all go. Regardless of the relationship between them, in which I have nothing to do at all. And maybe I should try to have a normal relationship with a normal girl.

The idea of working in Miranda's agency was terrible. I'm not like Michael, and I'm not like Stephen. She was right about this.

One thing is sure. That woman has a destructive influence. Michael bears his symptoms well, almost as if she had marked him. As if he was still dragging along the aftermath of an illness.

But I won't go beyond her borders and let myself be tempted and destroyed by her. Even if I started working in her crazy agency, I wouldn't let her manipulate me. Now that I understood her, I could pay attention and fight her. It's no longer possible for Michael. For him, it's already too late.

Miranda

Last night, I came home with a big headache. However, the meeting with Giles didn't go so badly. I thought it worse, even if, at first, it had taken an almost tragicomic turn. That boy eventually has a particular character; he's not passive and amorphous, as I had believed during the first appointment in the office.

I asked my secretary Kara to call Juliette and make an appointment for her in the afternoon. I didn't call her directly, or she would have tried to know something more. In this way, I kept her in suspense.

She arrives and scans me warily as if she doesn't know exactly what to expect from me. Stephen informed me of the outcome of their appointment immediately after escorting her to the front of her house.

I motion to her to sit in the chair before my desk. She nods but keeps looking at me with little conviction.

'I can schedule your friend's meeting with one of the boys.' I go straight to the other issue we had discussed, leaving out what concerns her directly. 'The first is free, then it depends on how many appointments she wants to book. However, you must still pay the registration fee.'

'Hmm... that boy whose picture you showed me last time?' She sighs and frowns. I'm surprised; I thought she was more interested in knowing my impression of her date with Stephen and my decision about it. 'He's nice, he could... yes, I think he could help Valerie. I will pay for the registration fee, of course. I can do it.'

'All right then, we can arrange a date between your friend and Giles.'

She nods again and looks away; she looks thoughtful, absorbed in other issues that only she knows.

'As far as you're concerned, however...' She doesn't seem interested, but I decide to inform her of my decision anyway. 'Stephen said you did very well, and it was nice to go out with you.'

Suddenly, she seems to turn away, to wake up. 'So... can I have the job?'

'Yes, but...' I pause and see her blue eyes widen on me, uncertain. 'Kara, my assistant, is moving to Australia with her boyfriend. I need someone to take her place. I know you have experience and already work for someone... and since you can deal well with people, as Stephen told me...'

I know, it's crazy. And Kara's moving is not so immediate. And maybe I'm infringing on gender equality. But a girl as a chaperone... no, I don't feel like it, not in my agency. Above all, she's not the right type.

'Are you offering me a job as your assistant?' She keeps staring at me sceptically. Would she have been less if I had planned her a date with an actual client?

'Yes, if you're interested, we can try it. Kara will still stay here a little bit and can instruct you.'

'It's different from what I thought. I mean... I'm grateful to you, but...' She bites her lips doubtfully, then intertwines her fingers and seems to meditate in search of the right words. 'I look for jobs with a flexible schedule because my real dream is another.'

'Of course, I understand. We could reach an agreement.'

'Hmm... why?' She sighs more deeply, squeezes her eyes, and looks at me seriously. I don't understand the sense of her question.

'Why what, Juliette?'

It doesn't bother her that I called her by her full name this time. She doesn't even seem to mind at all.

'Why do you want to help me? Why don't you want to give me a job as a chaperone, but you still want to offer me a chance?'

'Because, as I told you...' I sigh and cross my arms. I try to keep myself from losing patience. 'Kara will move soon, and I need someone to replace her. I'm just offering you a trial; you might not be suitable. Or the job may not be suitable for you.'

She leaves without giving me a precise answer. She says she'll think about it. I don't know what's on her mind, and I don't even care at this point.

It's almost teatime. And regularly, Raymond joins me, and he too looks at me strangely, lowering his glasses on his nose as if to look at me better.

'Tell me straight away what you have to say; don't beat around the bush about it.' I look at him firmly immediately after pouring the tea and the milk into the cups. I hand him one, sit at my desk and take a bar of chocolate from the top drawer.

'You wanted to help that girl.'

'Did you hide to listen to everything?' It's obvious. Today, however, they must stop highlighting my attempt to help someone. I'm usually not like that. And I don't even want to become like that.

'I was already here, just before she came in, and I happened to hear.' Raymond grabs his cup and takes small sips.

'You are never deaf when you feel like listening to something. Sure, you're not, Raymond?' I shake my head and roll my eyes.

'Very true! And I'm never blind when I want to see. Too bad you are too often, Miranda. Blind and deaf.'

'No, please. Not the lecture!' I pull back with the chair that is screeching unbearably. 'We've known each other too long now. You know I don't deserve it. And you also know that I'm a bitch and an opportunist exactly as I appear. That girl, Juliette... she really risks becoming a thorn in my side, that's why...'

As if I didn't already have enough excess baggage! Raymond stops sipping his tea and watches me intently, though his expression is now vaguely upset.

'You have a good heart; you don't want to take advantage of her. You should give more space to understanding in your life. And to love as well since you're dealing with it daily.'

'I'm dealing with an illusion of love. And of understanding, too. It's all fake; it doesn't exist. They pay to have it. Here, it's just some compliments and company, but there is no difference, really. There's nothing true. Maybe because it's just like that... there is nothing true.'

'No, I don't believe it, Miranda. And you don't believe either what you're saying.'

Raymond doesn't give me a break. I know how he is when something gets in his head. He knows how to be even more stubborn than me. To such an extent that it is often convenient to agree with him just to end the conversation. But not this time. Because I really want this conversation to end definitively. Once and for all. Because it would mean going back to thinking about the pain I buried inside, bringing it back to life and forcing myself to risk suffering it and endure it again... and again.

'There is nothing left. There was once, I admit it. I can't deny it. But now... There is only emptiness, Ray. I understand what you're trying to do for me, and I thank you. But it's useless. There is really nothing left in me. Only a void that nothing and nobody can ever fill.'

CHAPTER 17

Julie

I don't know how or why. I was inclined not to come back; it seemed crazy because I felt uncomfortable and constantly embarrassed with her. I'm here, however. The same evening, I called her to tell her I accepted her offer.

She asked me if I was available for a few hours the next day. That's why I'm here. Kara is instructing me, but it doesn't really seem complicated. She taught me to sort out the clients' requests and the guys they are intended for.

I didn't think that women turned to an agency like this. I'm appalled by the popularity of such an industry. Is it possible that many women of different ages find it difficult to find a chaperone? It's not even, in many cases, a matter of courtship or sex. Simple company. Professional, attentive, and often even discreet.

While Kara answers the phone, I inevitably dwell on the photographs of the boys. There are several of each. Among others, I recognize Stephen, of course. I observe some of his pictures and his indisputable physical prowess. Then Michael. Even in the photographs, he has a sulky expression, sometimes a little absent, as if he is lost and constantly thinking about something else. No, it's as if he has a massive chip on his shoulder with the whole world and intends to make it pay for some wrongs he has suffered. In other pictures, he smiles, but it looks more like a sneer than a smile.

Giles, finally. Only two of him. One looks like a passport photo. The other one seems destined explicitly for the agency.

He smiles and poses like a model, pulling on one of the sleeves of his sweater. But it shows that he's forced, not very spontaneous, really. I can almost imagine him; as soon as the lens is detached from him, he resumes his usual life and his natural expression. That natural expression has nothing to do with the photograph he presents to the clients; that one only serves to attract their interest in his face and body. Because I know he's something else. Much more.

Giles

She seemed to be waiting for me, and it really was the most absurd surprise that could have happened to me. She evidently knew that we would meet here. Of course, she knew if she was hired as an assistant to Miranda Crossing's assistant. So, among the other guys, she would have found me too.

I must say that the world is small. So, she found out that I had lied to her. Or rather, I kept part of the truth about my new job hidden.

I stopped by the "Secret Agents at Your Service" at Miranda's request, who would like to entrust me with my first assignment. Fortunately, she couldn't see my incredulous expression inside her office when I saw Julie sitting at the desk beside Kara.

'You will have your first assignment. But the girl knows nothing, so you must look natural. A chance meeting. I'll explain to you how we'll organize it.' Miranda's request comes as soon as I cross the threshold of her office. Only later, she greets me with a nod, gives me her usual forced smile and points me to the chair in front of her.

It doesn't seem this is in the terms, but I avoid pointing it out immediately. 'So, I'll have to pretend I'm really interested in her?' But I can't resist; I want explanations. 'I thought they were the clients who requested the agency's services.'

'That's usually the case, but this time...' Miranda frowns, only briefly. Then she shrugs. 'Don't go too far, though. It's only necessary to distract the girl a bit from an ex-boyfriend who's an as...'

'Asshole', I finish the sentence for her, not realizing that she didn't intend to utter the word in full; maybe she has just let herself be dragged beyond her rigidity and coldness.

'Exactly.'

'But if...' If the girl deluded herself that I was really interested in a relationship with her, wouldn't it be even worse?

'I understand what you mean. Try to cheer her up a little, but don't make her fall in love. That's why I thought that you...'

Once again, she avoids continuing. Basically, she's rubbing it in my face that I can be good as a diversion to cheer up and distract a poor abandoned girl, but it's practically impossible to fall in love with me. But thanks, Miranda Crossing! She couldn't have made it clearer to me than this! Michael is right. She's a bitch!

'Don't get me wrong, Giles.' Evidently, she has understood and is trying to repair the damage.

'No, don't worry. I understood very well.' Yes, I really understood very well. And now I'll fix her! 'Why didn't you ask Michael? He's much better than me at "distracting"'.

'Michael? What does he have to do with it?' I see her blushing, even though she desperately tries to compose herself.

Then there really is something underneath. Actually, I had no idea what to say and how to drag my cousin into the middle, but I wanted to do it. Just to challenge her and observe her reaction. Now, I'm the one amusing myself by seeing her in evident difficulty.

'Michael is busy elsewhere.' She ends it without giving me any further explanation. 'I will let you know the precise details of how to organize the meeting with Valerie. The girl's name is Valerie.'

And so, she dismisses me with an unhappy and bored expression. I don't like this setup, and maybe I should express my disappointment, refuse, and disappear. I would do it right now. But things have changed. Julie is here. And I want to find out something more about her. And on this absurd coincidence that, after letting us meet, dragged us both here.

I stop to greet her. Since I had arrived just in time for the appointment with Miranda, I couldn't talk to her.

'It's really a strange coincidence', I smile as I approach her side of the desk.

'No, not really. I found the flyers in the Trasks' shop; I became curious and...' Julie wrinkles her nose in a funny but beautiful, irresistible expression.

'Did you want a guy for Valentine's Day?' It seems strange to me, and I would like to tell her she could find one without going to an agency. But I'm afraid that she misinterprets my words.

'No, no. Actually, I was just very curious... and it happened that they were looking for help for the assistant who is going to move, so...'

'Of course, everything is clear.' Not really, but it doesn't matter. 'Anyway, I left the flyers at the Trasks. No, it was my cousin, Michael, actually. So, if it wasn't just a coincidence, it's definitely a strange twist of fate.'

CHAPTER 18

Miranda

I approached the door ajar, and I listened to them. Yes, sure. Coincidence or strange twist of fate. The world is very small; despite its size, Dublin sometimes feels like a village. So, these two came here to me through advertising flyers that I wasn't even particularly keen to get created and spread around by Michael and Stephen.

And the most absurd issue is that they're obviously interested in each other. But she doesn't seem to notice it and is seriously intent on getting him to go out with her best friend. People are crazy, really. I, however, who indulges them, am no less!

I call Juliette in my office with an excuse.

'So, what is your purpose exactly? Push Giles to go out with your friend. And do you also want him to court her?'

'He seems like a good guy to me.' She replies without much emphasis, as if she had already studied the sentence. 'Valerie doesn't know anything, and anyway, I thought we agreed. I'll pay what I owe, of course.'

'Yes, but now the situation seems to have changed a little. You know Giles, you've met before. Don't deny it. And anyway, there won't be any romance between them; it seems obvious to me. So, it could all end with your friend feeling even worse than she is now.'

'Maybe I shouldn't have, but... it seemed like a good idea to distract her a little from her sadness and from the fact that maybe she would like to leave, so...' she sighs and bites her lips nervously. I think she's the first to doubt her own idea, but she doesn't want to hold back, probably on principle. 'Now we just have to wait for Giles to meet Valerie and see what happens between them.'

A disaster, that's what will happen! I don't say this openly, but most of the time, I'm unable to control my facial expression.

'You're manipulating people's lives, Juliette. Maybe not Giles', who is aware of the plan. Even if he doesn't know yet that it's your friend. And Valerie, who is totally in the dark...' I shake my head; I feel that we're about to walk towards a spiral of misunderstandings and endless misconceptions, mainly because Giles' interest is clearly directed elsewhere. 'I suggest you mention something to your friend before she discovers your scheming. Or you'll end up finding yourself with disappointed expectations, a lost friend and a guy who believes you don't care about him at all.'

That's it, I said it. But Juliette stares at me dejected and disgruntledly, especially after my last words.

'Hmm...' She doesn't express anything else; she nods and retires as soon as I let her understand that I've finished with her.

But then... if life and love really are part of a game, of an infinite plan, maybe I should start playing too, just like Juliette. Apparently, I misunderstood. Her interest in Giles is purely superficial; otherwise, she wouldn't let him go that way. For me, it's different. I have no choice; now my time has passed, finished, and expired.

I take my cell phone and stare at it for a moment. Then I select the number, and I send a message. I stand up, put on my jacket, and take my bag.

'I must go out for an errand; I'll be out for a few hours.' I turn to Juliette; Kara asked me for permission to leave a little earlier to catch the train to Galway and visit her parents. 'Do you think I can leave you alone to answer the phone? We're not waiting for anyone, anyway.'

'Yes, sure. No problem.' Julie, busy sorting the old mail, looks up at me.

I feel like my stomach is gripping, but I'm convinced it's the right choice. At least it's an attempt.

'Good…' I still hesitate in the doorway before leaving. 'If there are any problems, you can call me on my cell phone or turn to Raymond, who lives on the first floor. But I'm sure everything will be fine.'

Michael

I arrive at Miranda as soon as possible, even though I was on the opposite side of the city. She didn't specify whether she meant her office or her home. Given the time, I imagine she's in her office. But I first look for her at home and ring the bell several times. Uselessly.

I have a copy of the agency's keys; I enter without ringing. I notice someone spying on my movements, but I pretend nothing happened. Raymond, as always. I'm sure he already knows everything for a long time.

She's not here. Apparently, she went out for an errand. Julie, sitting at the entrance desk, looks at me, puzzled. I'm afraid I scared her when I entered without ringing.

I wonder why the hell Miranda sent me that somewhat cryptic message asking me to reach her here as soon as possible. When I tried to call her then, her cell phone was unreachable. Why did she get me here knowing she had to leave?

'She said she'd be back, anyway.' Even Julie looks confused and uncomfortable.

I observe her carefully. Yes, it was really a bizarre coincidence to find her here again. She roughly explains to me how things went; she says she found the flyers at the Trasks' shop. I pretend to believe her; in fact, I don't even care.

I feel like an idiot for how I rushed here as soon as I received her message when she didn't even bother responding to my following message or my call.

'If you want, you can wait for her; I'm sure she will come back.' Julie smiles, looking kind, but I'm not in the mood. 'Do you want tea? Or a coffee?'

'I know where they are; I would do it myself if I wanted it. I wouldn't ask you.' I reply brusquely, and I don't even notice it. Indeed, yes. But only following the dismayed expression on her face. 'Sorry... what I wanted to say is that you're not obliged to make me coffee or tea.'

'Yes, I understand.' She nods and smiles slightly, but I notice that she doesn't particularly like my company.

I'm mad at Miranda, not at her. But I can't tell her. It may be better for me to get out of the way, so it seems clear that Her Majesty Queen Miranda won't have the courtesy of returning for me. She made fun of me again.

'I'll call Miranda later.' I make up an excuse that it's not even an excuse. But just a way to vanish, giving a kind of explanation. 'Thank you, Julie. I hope to see you again.'

'Sure.' She smiles more openly, maybe grateful that I'm going to remove my bulky and unfriendly disturbance.

Meanwhile, I meditate on the crap I just said: "I hope to see you again." And why should I hope for it? Okay, it's better not to think about it too much. Surely, she had already forgotten it or wasn't even listening to me.

If Miranda really thinks about getting rid of me like that or fucking me around, she's wrong. What did she try to do? Why did she look for me when she almost completely ignored me for days, if not weeks now? And when she talks to me or we have to meet, she always makes sure that someone else is present.

So, no way, I'm not leaving. I have decided to wait for her, but not at the agency. Because I know she will come back. She has no other choice.

I order a coffee and sit in front of the window of the coffee shop on the other side of the street from her home. I could wait for her for hours, I know. But this time, we will arrive at a definitive clarification. She will have to stop playing with me. Stop ignoring me and pretending nothing happened. She can't lock me up in a drawer, too. She will have to stop it, once and for all.

CHAPTER 19

Miranda

I behaved like a fool, I know. What did I hope to achieve? I saw his message and his call. Then another message, another again... another call. I enticed him to me by writing to him that we had to talk about something important. I didn't specify what and which part of our complicated relationship.

I acted instinctively, asking him to reach me, and I was wrong; it's clear to me now. Because I really didn't want anything I had planned to happen. And immediately afterwards, I left before he arrived. I acted exactly like Juliette, in short. I was imitating a script written by her.

As I reached the centre, I started wandering through the courtyards of Trinity College, then to Temple Bar, to the delightful Market Arcade on South Great George Street, the ancient covered market which is one of my favourite places in Dublin and usually makes me feel better, physically, and morally. I wasted some time chatting with the merchants; I bought a silver necklace and two books about Dublin's history. While nothing could really get my attention, the cold became increasingly bitter. So, I took refuge in the cafeteria of the Irish Film Institute on Eustace Street.

While I was holed up sipping hot chocolate and deciding whether I wanted to watch a movie, I called Raymond, asking him to close the agency for me and let Juliette go home. A few hours later, I returned directly to my home. I had the feeling of a shadow behind me, someone following me.

I thought I was wrong, but I wasn't. And I also thought he was gone. I was wrong. I panic, and I feel a tension that I can't control. Fortunately, I managed to get into my house before he reached me, pretending not to hear his footsteps, his voice behind me.

I hope he resigns and leaves. But I know him too well by now. In fact, as I lean against the wall in a state of disorientation that I can't control, I hear the bell ring. He doesn't just press it; he seems more like hitting it with all the strength and anger he has in his body.

I sigh and hold my chest as if my heart could explode at any moment. What have I done? And why? I only helped make the situation even tenser. I was childish and foolish. I shouldn't have given in, even before. I never should have; I knew it was wrong. And now I can't open to him, let him in.

I stay still in the dark, constantly leaning against the wall. I wait for him to get tired and decide to stop, to go away. In fact, he finally gives up. I close my eyes and run my hands on my face. I don't feel like facing him even if I realize I've been looking for it this time. Not now.

'Miranda!'

In the silence of the evening and of my house, his voice makes me jump. I press my hand to my lips as if I had to force myself to hold my breath so as not to answer.

'Miranda! I know you're there; I've seen you!' He raises his voice even more. Shortly after, he starts banging on my door. 'It was you looking for me, Miranda! Open this fucking door, damn it!'

I move towards the centre of the entrance, and I look at the door as if it were my worst enemy. He won't give up; he knows I'm here. And it's not his character to give up, even if only on principle. However, I remain silent. I close my eyes, almost as if I could see him beyond the barrier that separates us and that a part of me would like to break down.

'Miranda! Miranda!' Now he's really screaming. And he also kicked the door.

Neighbours will undoubtedly be hearing him, too. I can imagine them. Hushed and at the windows, their eyes turned towards my house, my door. And towards him.

'Michael... go away!' I barely whisper; I don't even know if I want him to hear me. 'Please, go away.'

'Open, Miranda...' His voice tones down and softens. But it's only an illusion because he returns to knock with the same impetus as before. 'It was you who sought me out! Why?'

'Stop punching the door, Michael. Everybody will hear you!'

'And who is this everybody? Like I give a shit about everybody!'

I get precisely the opposite effect. I should have guessed it, knowing him. Michael is vehement, disrespectful, and stubborn. Unstoppable and obstinate, as if he was animated by a constant fire. The same fire that ignited me, too.

'You don't behave like that here... neighbours...' I'm thinking about my good name, my neighbourhood. When I don't even think I have a good name to uphold, let alone a neighbourhood I care about.

I take a few steps away, determined to take refuge in my room and forget his presence beyond my door. Unexpectedly, he has decided to let it go, too; he stops calling me and beating the door.

I go back. I stop a few steps from the entrance. With a deep breath, I put my hand on the handle. Then I suddenly open it before I can rethink and change my mind.

He's still here. Motionless in front of me. And he looks at me with an expression so disappointed and embittered that it hurts me. He doesn't move or even try to get in now. His green eyes have a new light, intense and vibrant. They shine in the darkness of the evening and are focused on me, on my face.

I continue staring at him with the same disquieting desolation, as if there was nothing left to do, to say.

'Why, Miranda?' He shrugs, then runs a hand through his hair. 'All right, I got it. You don't behave like that here... neighbours...'

He steps back, and then he turns; he walks a few steps towards the road.

'No, Michael...'

I follow him and stretch out my arms to hold him. Even if being turned away, he couldn't see me. Do I have to let him go? I must...

'I wanted you... to meet Juliette. That you tried with her... to know her, to...'

'Why, do you think I can't find myself a girl... or two... or ten without your encouragement? Without your scheming? Do you really believe I couldn't go out with another woman, have fun, sleep with her?' He turns around but lifts his face towards the sky. 'That's not the point. But it's useless trying to explain what you obviously can't understand. You're done playing with me this time. Goodbye, Miranda.'

'No, I...'

I got what I wanted. Let him go. Even if not Juliette or someone else. He let me go and decided to say goodbye and get out of my life. My life, which he entered many years ago, step by step. He was so young, so bold. When I was almost completely destroyed. He was the one I wanted with a desire that had never happened to me before, with anyone.

'Michael!'

It's me now screaming his name while he's already hurrying away from me. It's me walking the distance that separates us and then freezing when he suddenly stops and turns his face towards me. With his eyes so bright that they break my heart.

I feel a tear prick my eye insistently. Only one, the left one. I try to block it, but it runs down my cheek. Even if I quickly stop all its tracks with my hand. I close my eyes to halt the others, too. Or maybe not to see him go away from me.

Instead, suddenly, I feel tightened. I sigh and lean my head back. Just when his lips are searching for mine. I grab him by his nape and abandon myself to his kiss, his mouth exploring mine. I allow myself to long for his body to return to life.

Indifferent to those watching us, I continue to kiss him, returning home in his arms. As he closes the door, he goes down to kiss my neck, and his hands grab me and run over me greedily, with a frenzy I can't resist.

I can't have him, I know. It's not fair; he's not for me. But I can't lose him or let him go completely. Because I know that if it happened, I'd lose myself too. That part of myself I'm still trying to protect, to save.

Michael

Everything happens as in a scene already lived. In fact, it's a scene already lived and retraced at least a thousand times in my mind. And I really wanted to end it this time. Tell her to go to hell. Even if I already know what happens then. Even if I already know, it's not the conclusion of everything between us. There is no end, neither happy nor tragic. But this continuous taking each other, grabbing each other, holding each other, possessing each other.

This is always how it has been with her for too many years. And then allow her to return to grieve and despair over that photograph she keeps in her drawer. And it's there, again, to remind her that I'm not enough. That she's not for me. And in doubt, vent the frustration on the chocolate she keeps hidden in another drawer.

I know you well, Miranda. I despise you when you don't give you and me a chance. An "us".

I continue to kiss her with more sweetness now, mixed with a passion that I can never restrain when she's in front of me, when she calls me.

She breaks away, and her breathing labours as I press my body against hers.

'Michael...'

She holds me by the edge of my jacket with both her hands. I look into her eyes. Her fear, the desperation that makes her so fragile and vulnerable, makes me afraid of shattering her by only holding her a little tighter.

I nod and pull away from her. Yes, it's a scene repeated so many times. Not exactly the same. Not like this, maybe. Not always here. But the feelings are the same.

'All right, Miranda. I understand. I won't touch you again.'

At least for tonight. Or maybe forever. And in the end, I really would like it. So much that perhaps I'll try. To look for another woman, someone like Juliette. Why not just Juliette? I would have nothing to lose. Just this feeling of constant abandonment, of never being enough for her... this feeling that gives me, every time, my obsession for Miranda Crossing.

CHAPTER 20

Julie

Summarizing the most favourable conditions and leaving out the most embarrassing parts, I told Valerie about my new job. Obviously, I avoid telling her what I'm planning and the part that concerns her and involves her directly. I also show her the "infamous" flyer and the sentence that attracts her attention as well.

"Why not live a fairytale week with a man who venerates you and makes you feel like the most beautiful and desired woman on the love feast?"

'But it's really bizarre...' She makes a sceptical grimace. 'How did you find it?'

'It was a chance, a coincidence.' A coincidence that I helped to create, but it doesn't matter now. 'The kind of situation intrigued me; it amused me, and I went there for fun. And they were just looking for an assistant to replace Kara, who is about to move. So... it happened!'

'Yeah, sometimes the strangest situations happen.' And strangely enough, in fact, she believes me. Why would she doubt, anyway? 'It still seems crazy, but at least it will be fun. Even if... in short, it doesn't seem like a great idea to go out with someone and be courted like that. It's absurd that some women are fine with having false attention, a simulated interest. I mean, I'd never do that! It would all be a staging, a scam.'

'Yes, sure. You're right. Obviously, it's all a game... but at least it's a distraction; it could certainly be fun for those who want something different. A bit like in "women only" or bridal shower parties.'

I bite my lips. I should have avoided referencing anything that could remind her of a possible marriage. But Valerie is not at all upset about it; in fact, she doesn't even seem to notice my involuntary gaffe.

'You're right; it could even be fun.' She smiles and nods, then chuckles and looks at me suspiciously. 'Have you already met someone interesting, by any chance? Since you work there…'

'Oh, no. No one for me, absolutely no one!' I pledge to deny it with all my strength. And I rightly pointed out "for me". 'I don't even think I could go out with other agency employees or deal with them personally.'

I really don't know. Neither Miranda nor others mentioned this impediment to me as if it was a kind of conflict of interest. Don't go out with colleagues. However, our assignments are completely different.

But it's not necessary. I create the impediment. Because it's not good, in short. Because I have other plans in this regard. And I won't let anyone get in the way, not even myself. Because, above all, I know how it turns out every damn time. I know from experience.

Giles

Stopping by the agency to leave some of my pictures and other advertising flyers created by Michael is a good excuse. I could have sent everything by e-mail. And then there was nothing urgent. They were not even necessary.

Anyone would understand that this is an excuse. But I don't care. The truth is that I wanted to see her again. I wasn't even sure she was there; I had to take a chance.

She looks at me and smiles, a little perplexed; maybe she didn't expect to see me. In part, she seems annoyed by my presence. Or she's embarrassed, but I don't understand the reason. Maybe having discovered my new job, even though I haven't really started yet, makes her feel uncomfortable. Because of how I talked about it, she surely imagined something different.

'Would you like to have lunch with me?' I ask her the question without overthinking.

She looks up from her desk while pretending to concentrate on a register where I believe all the meetings, the clients' names, the places, and the agreed prices are pinned.

'It's... early.' She hesitated. She had to think about it, and I don't understand why. She lowers her eyes for a moment, almost disappointed. Then she looks back at me and smiles with a little lacklustre smile.

'All right. We can wait if you want to go later.' I raise my arm, and I look absently at my watch. 'Sooner or later, Miranda will let you take a break, right?'

Actually, Miranda is locked in her office, from which the slightest movement doesn't come. I know she's there because Julie went in to deliver what I had brought to her. I thought she called and wanted to talk to me, but she's completely ignoring my presence here. They're both strange, then.

'No, actually...' she sighs, shrugs, and stands up. 'We can go even now. Miranda said I can take a break when I want today. In any case, Kara will be here soon.'

Now, she smiles more openly and puts her jacket on. She moves towards Miranda's office and knocks on the door only twice, lightly. She enters, and she leaves almost immediately. I observe her slender figure, the blue and black pleated skirt that, despite not being too short, shows off her slender but well-shaped legs.

I look up at her face as she turns to me. We walk out without knowing exactly where to go; I still don't know the area well. We both look around. Julie points to a small house with a green roof and an oriental sign on the window.

'It's a Chinese restaurant if you like.' She gives me a more open smile and then wraps herself tightly in her jacket. 'I've been there before; it's quite good.'

I accept and follow her without question; it's not for the food that I invited her for lunch. The restaurant is self-service, and we are quickly seated at the table between egg fried rice, shrimp balls, almond chicken, and spring rolls.

'I started to mention the idea to Valerie...' Julie deliberately leaves the sentence hanging, but I won't encourage her to tell me about her friend. So, she's obliged to continue. 'On Miranda's suggestion. Then I don't know how... well, I couldn't keep it hidden from her that I'm working at the agency.'

'Why?' I sigh and stare at her. Actually, I'm not even particularly hungry today. 'I mean... why did you start working in Miranda's agency? I know you found the flyers, but there are so many other jobs.'

'I was curious and wanted to help Valerie, as you already know. But then I also thought of...' she half-closes her eyes for a moment and bites her lips. She straightens her back and places her forearms on the table. 'Now I don't know what you'll think, but... okay, you can think whatever you want, but initially, I asked Miranda to hire me for the same job that you do. Going out with clients, even if the agency has no male clients; I asked her to think about it. I did it for money because I need it for my cooking classes. I want to become a food blogger more than anything else; I've already explained it to you. And I thought I would also have enough time available with this job. I still work as Sarah Ward's assistant, even if I start to fear that I will never

126

learn enough and I won't become a good food blogger like her. Miranda told me she would think about it, but then... she decided to hire me for another job, let's say. So here I am.'

'I believe that if that's exactly what you want to do in life, you will succeed.' Just a cliché. Quite bad, so much so that it reminds me of very cheap self-help manuals. Think positive. If you want, you can. Believe it with all your heart. Except that, it's not always like that, unfortunately. I decide to gloss over the subject and move on to a topic of greater interest, at least for me. 'Why do you want your friend to go out with someone at all costs? After all, she could find someone by herself, don't you think?'

'Yes, she will do it sooner or later. I thought I'd cheer her up a bit right now. I wanted her to stop thinking about her ex and suffering for him, even if...' she snorts in dismay, then points her blue eyes at me. Almost as if I was the main cause of her disappointment. 'You still agree, don't you?'

'Of course, if that's what you want from me. I'll go out with your friend Valerie. I'll do my best to make her have fun and feel good. If this is what Miranda orders me to do and what you ask me, I'll do it.'

CHAPTER 21

Miranda

I've been sitting at my office desk for hours. Staring into space. Without concluding anything. Indifferent to everything. Juliette came in and left me something; I nodded without listening to what she told me.

Because there's only him in my head. I sent him away just when I would have given anything to hold him and not let him go anymore. His arms around me, his lips almost devouring me, his body against mine. I feel quivering at the thought of him, as always, when I see him. And I was really going to surrender one more time after deciding that it would never happen again.

Michael crept into my life day after day, look after look. And what upsets me is that I knew it right away. Although he was much younger and I was still tied to someone else, even though the relationship with my ex-husband had come to an end because of his infidelities and my decision to stop forgiving him. The truth that I have never been able to admit, not even to myself, is that in the meantime, I also started to think about someone else within my own mind. But I would have tried to control myself, to restrain myself.

I should have found a way to send Michael away, not let him take over my will and senses. Instead, I did precisely the opposite. I kept him with me. For me. While he was going out with other women for work. And then some other women, because his private life didn't belong to me and doesn't belong to me.

There are many other guys in the agency, there have been. It has never happened with anyone. I had some adventures with men who had nothing to do with my work; I tried to establish relationships that were wrecked one after the other, but never with my employees. He has been the only one, although I'm convinced enough that he believes the opposite.

But what does it matter to me anyway what he believes? I must find a way to push him away. I sent him away. I think back to the scene, and not even a fragment of the memory of his skin, of his fragrance on me, escapes me. Of his anger and my torment that we haven't been able to control. But in the end, I succeeded. I stopped him, and I sent him away, really. So why is he still here, with me, in my mind, in my breaths? More present than ever.

'You can send me away as much as you want, Miranda.' The words he addressed to me, without anger, without harshness anymore. In his shining eyes, perhaps wrongly, I could only read regret and desolation. 'You will never get out of the situation you got into because the truth is that you don't want to get out. I'm not the problem.'

'Then really go away, this time. Leave it all behind, don't ever come back.' With every word I spoke, my heart pounded in my chest, contradicting and denying all my hardness, my severity. But by now, I had become irreducible, ruthless. 'Leave the agency too. I accept your resignation.'

'I can do it if you want.' His eyes shot arrows at me. But I remained firmly protected by my imperturbable armour. 'I never gave a damn about your agency.'

'Yeah, you always did it for the money. I always knew that.'

'This is where you're wrong, Miranda.' He shook his head and then slowly turned, ready to leave, to disappear from my life. I could no longer see him, even though I had a great need to see him. 'I could have other jobs; I have another job now that doesn't involve escorting women I don't care about. I've stopped doing it for money a long time ago. I did it for you.'

Julie

'If you really insist, I'll give it a try! But you know very well that I've never liked these "blind dates".' Valerie gives me a decidedly sceptical grimace. 'So don't deceive yourself that something will happen between me and your new friend Giles.'

I told her about Giles and that she could go out with him just to do something different. I didn't tell her everything, really. Giles is just a guy I met and made friends with. I met him at Trasks while I was picking up Sarah's computer, and then he solved my problem of it not being repaired. I totally omitted any connection between Giles and Miranda's agency.

'All right, I'm sure you won't regret it.'

Valerie looks at me and smiles. Giles is really her type. So peaceful, so sweet. No, maybe not always. And now he does a truly unconventional job, but...

'Tell me why you don't go out with him if he's so special.'

Special? When and where did I say that I consider him special? Valerie seems to read my mind because she immediately answers my silent question.

'You never have such positive judgments about men. If you insist, there must be a reason. You have only known him recently; you cannot have become such good friends already!'

'Why not? In short, we immediately connected and...' And I don't know how to proceed. I feel uncomfortable, not only with Val but also with Giles, who is not even here.

'That's it; you've got to the point, Julie. If you feel so good with him and have created this incredible connection, why don't you go out with him?'

CHAPTER 22

Giles

Sooner or later, I had to start. At this point better with a pretty girl. Because Valerie is very pretty. Blonde and with big bright eyes, perfect features, and a lovely facial expression. But I can hardly consider her as a woman with whom I could have a relationship.

I would have let it go if I could. Whether as a personal favour to Julie or as a job for the agency. Especially since Valerie thinks I'm just a friend of Julie, who insisted on us getting to know each other. She used it as an excuse that we were both disappointed by relationships that ended badly. A more pathetic excuse she couldn't make up without even knowing that, in my case, it's the truth. And then finished relationships almost always end badly, at least for one of the two.

Miranda recommended that I behave impeccably and make the girl feel special. Special is one of the most absurd words in the world. It means everything and nothing; most of the time, it's used when you don't know what to say or how to define something. From the expression Miranda used with me, I believe she's aware of it, too. Maybe she used it specifically for this reason. To say everything and the opposite of everything. This is my first assignment for the "Secret Agents at Your Service" agency. And Valerie isn't even a regular client; she doesn't know how it works. She came across this strange world, just like me.

So, I find myself with Valerie in a city centre Italian restaurant located along the Ha'penny Bridge, South of the city. We talk a little about this and that, the trivial dialogues that are usually made to get to know each other, but without going too far. Where do you come from, what do you do for a living, how long have you lived here... Once we know we are both "foreigners", we discuss the Irish lifestyle and what we like to do in our spare time.

I don't know if I'm making her feel special; I'm trying to do my best to get to know her. But from the expression she's giving me, she is feeling more bored than special. Then, having exhausted the "typical" subjects of the first date, she talks to me about Julie. Obviously, she is the person we have in common who convinced us to try this date. Valerie's French accent is much more pronounced than Julie's. I speak slowly, fearing that she must struggle to understand me.

'I've known Julie since we were children in France. Although she has always lived in Geneva.'

'So, did you move here together?' I follow the conversation without much interest. Or rather, hoping to change the subject without being able to think of something better.

Julie is the main reason why I'm here now. With another woman, as my job for the agency requires. But the woman in question is also her friend, so it's more like a private favour. Which, in this case, does nothing but highlight Julie's disinterest in me.

'Not really, but I wouldn't know what to do here without her. I lived a somewhat complicated period a few months ago.' Valerie sighs and looks into my eyes, tilting her face. 'Am I boring you? Or is my accent so terrible, and you can't understand what I'm saying?'

'No, I understand you very well. And I find your accent really nice.' I was clutching at straws to try to justify my blatant carelessness.

I'm a failure both as a friend and as a professional suitor. If Valerie were an actual agency client, she would have to bring everything back to Miranda and insist that she fire me!

'But not as nice as Julie's, sure it isn't?' Valerie smiles amusedly, maybe for the first time during the evening.

I smile, too; I can't do anything else. And I try to recover and save what can be saved, as well as throwing Valerie off the truth. 'Actually, Julie's accent is barely perceptible. And yours, I must admit, is much more fascinating.'

'Giles...' Valerie bites her lips and reaches for me from her side of the table. 'You can even stop pretending; I know what's underneath. I know about Julie's work at the agency and... I mean, it's clear that you are one of the "St Valentine's Secret Agents", even though she passed you off as a friend she met by chance in the appliance store. It seems obvious to me.'

It would be useless to lie now. The girl got there easily. Maybe, in fact, it wasn't so complicated to figure it out.

'The truth is that I met Julie before we both joined the agency...' I confess quietly as Valerie finally seems interested in the conversation. 'So, we're really friends, regardless of work. I mean, my date with you is more a request from Julie than an appointment with a client. And in any case... I'm just a beginner; I've just started. In fact, you are my first.'

'I confess that this "famous" agency is also intriguing me,' she declares calmly. 'Even if at the beginning, when Julie told me about it, I found it a very absurd idea.'

'I apologize, anyway. I'm afraid this job won't do for me,' I sigh, laying my eyes on the plate before me, then lifting them on her. 'They should have sent you a more experienced professional agent.'

'No, I really don't think so. Indeed, it would have been worse.' Valerie seems to relax even more now that part of the matter is cleared up. And I'm no longer forced to pretend. 'I agreed to please Julie. She's convinced I'm still suffering for my ex, Trent.'

'And you're not?'

'Not the same way anymore.' She shakes her head decisively, then sips a little white wine from the glass before her. 'I tried to explain it to Julie, but I'm afraid she didn't believe me.'

'Julie can be really stubborn; I noticed it.'

'The truth is another, Giles. She's suffering much more than me from what happened to her in the past.' Valerie entwines her fingers and stares at me now with a severe expression. 'I got over it by now. Indeed, I'm convinced that it was good that Trent left me a few weeks before the wedding. It would have been a mistake for me.'

'Yes, I understand very well what you mean. As for me, there was no talk of marriage yet, but I had a very similar experience.'

She tells me about her history with Trent. And, strangely, I can tell something about myself as well as I've never done before out of fear or maybe out of shame. I get rid of the burden of my past life, along with her. The evening takes a very different turn from what I had predicted and, I believe, from what Julie had planned for us. I realize that Valerie is quiet about her past, even if it's such a recent past. Maybe she still feels slightly angry at the ex, but she is letting it slip on her now.

In any case, Valerie is right. Julie is the one who suffers, regrets and doesn't let go. It's Julie who cannot get rid of her past pain, of the sense of desolation, of abandonment. And I'm afraid she won't seek any help. Not from me. Julie is so attached to her past that she cannot live in her present. Maybe because her present could be me. Maybe because she needs a present that interests her more than I do.

Julie

'So, how did it go?'

I try to find out something from Giles, as Valerie came back last night with a dreamy expression, but I couldn't get a word out of her more than a condescending "good".

'Very good!' After adding the milk, he smiles as he stirs the tea I just made for him.

From him, I managed to get only a "very", just one word more. The cases are two: either the evening was a disaster, and they agreed not to let me feel too bad by giving me the same version of the facts, or... the evening went too well. An irresistible attraction was unleashed between them, and they made sparks. Valerie was back after midnight, and I was already in my bedroom. It didn't seem appropriate to go out to question her, so I waited until the morning. But if they really had sparks, maybe she would have spent the night with him... or maybe not...

'So, will you go out with Val again?'

'Why not?'

Giles gives me another cryptic reply, looks away from me and hints at Kara, who has just returned from her lunch break. Stephen arrives right behind her. Kara has a strangely excited expression. Maybe it's Stephen who has this effect on her. Even though she's engaged and she's moving to Australia with her future husband. Maybe she has an attraction for Australians. I'm not even sure that Kara's fiancé is Australian, but...

But why are Val and Giles refusing to talk to me about their evening? Maybe something happened between them, and they don't dare tell me. Or do they want to wait...? I don't know; maybe they prefer to know each other better before they go too far. So that means the plan worked, and Val doesn't suspect that Giles works for this agency. But then, if she finds out...

'Hey, beautiful! Are you daydreaming?' Stephen swings his hand in front of my eyes to ensure I'm awake. I was so distracted that I didn't even notice that he was standing before me. 'Don't you greet the old selectors?'

He catches me off guard, and even Giles and Kara laugh at me and the almost catatonic state in which I fell. Fortunately, Giles doesn't suspect he was at the centre of my "daydream".

I tilt my head and smile at Stephen. 'Hi, old selector.'

I can partly take the thought of Giles and Valerie from my mind. Or at least I try to file it for the moment. I would have never believed it, but I'm starting to feel at home in the agency. It's a world of its own, in a way. But even my relationship with Miranda is very different from that with Sarah. I work for both, but Miranda, while often cynical and dry in her attitude, treats me more like a person with thoughts, interests, and feelings. For Sarah, all thoughts, interests and feelings are primarily her own. It doesn't matter what I think or want. What I may need is not her problem because I must live according to the achievement of her goals and her well-being when I am with her.

I met most of the boys I had previously identified only in photos and records inserted in the computer. These last few days have become more hectic than the previous ones, maybe due to the approach of Valentine's Day. It's funny to think of them as "secret agents", but now I can hardly help it. They stop by to talk to Miranda and to make arrangements about the clients. It still seems a bit absurd, out of this world, but somehow real.

I also met and got to know Raymond better, the owner of the building. He almost always stops by for five o'clock tea. He's a kind and sweet man, an old friend of Miranda's aunt.

Then there is her, whose path I cross every day. And every day, she promises me love and happiness. I discovered her name, Tally. Everyone knows her here. She's always in the same place; she shelters under the arcade when it rains. She resists despite being so thin and delicate. She resists time in every sense. Maybe when so many storms have crossed your life, you become resistant to everything, even to a bit of rain and wind. And, although they told me little about her, although I never really stopped to talk to her, and I don't know her story, I have the impression that the tender, fragile Tally has gone through so many storms in her life.

CHAPTER 23

Miranda

He takes advantage of the moment I allowed the others to go to the cafeteria to face me. Besides, I needed a bit of solitude and silence. The boys manage to create enough confusion when they come here in twos or threes at the same time. But I have the feeling of being almost boxed into a corner. And I don't like it.

'I haven't seen him around here for a while. Not when you're here, let's say.' Raymond also looks around to trace his statement even more. As if I hadn't already understood who he was referring to. 'So, I'm afraid you haven't resolved the situation with him yet.'

'He might have other stuff to do. Maybe better stuff,' I reply, bored, looking for something useless among the papers I have on my desk. Just not to look at him or let him read the desolation and melancholy in my eyes.

'You know it's not true. And anyway, inside, you hope it's not true.' He sighs, shakes his head, and sits beside me.

I get up to prepare our usual tea, hoping to distract him and be able to change the subject. I concentrate on turning the kettle on, placing the cups on the shelf, and putting one bag in each as if it were an operation to be performed with extreme care and caution. I always focus on making tea when I want to avoid a discussion.

'I'm late preparing for the usual party; I hope to find someone who helps me out. You will be there, won't you, Ray?'

I turn to him for a moment, and I close my eyes to be able to think about something else. Something that is not what has tormented me for days. Something like the usual party. The party I organize on Valentine's Day is for people who don't have someone to share their life with. Not a real love, in the most common sense of the term. Another tradition that was transferred by Aunt Grace and I haven't yet managed to eradicate.

'Why don't you love again, Miranda? Why don't you give that guy a chance?'

As I feared, my attempt to divert the subject elsewhere didn't help. Knowing Raymond, I suspected it. I must be firm and determined to induce him to resign. He has always managed to convince me on several issues. But he will have to give up on this.

'Because I already know the end. And I prefer not to live or experience it firsthand,' I reply firmly. 'I don't want to. I like my life the way it is, Ray. I finally reached stability. Or rather, a respite from everything I have endured in my past. I really don't want my situation to change. So, I can't...'

'You risk losing something beautiful, something important.'

Raymond listened to me in silence for too long. I waited for his interruption, in fact. But he won't make me change my mind; I will never change my mind. I must safeguard myself because I'm certain that no one else will do it for me.

'Do you think I don't know? I know.' I close my eyes and run my hands over my face. I'm tired, infinitely tired. I suffer from chronic fatigue that doesn't allow me to rest well, even when I should and would like to. And he has been helping keep me from sleeping for several nights. 'I also tried to convince myself that everything would be fine. But it's impossible; I have no hope. I haven't had any with my ex-husband, let alone with a guy like Michael.'

'You have too many prejudices. Not all people are the same. Michael is young, but he's not your ex-husband. You are not the same, either. It's another story, another life. And you're denying yourself to live it with a man who could make you happy. The fact that he's younger doesn't mean anything. It's not the age that determines a person.'

Raymond's speech strikes me but doesn't reach me unexpectedly. Because it's the same that I've been repeating to myself for too long. But now, hearing it from someone else, from him in particular, has an even more devastating effect on me. He could make me happy. I know. He has already made me happy. Every time I'm in his arms, I forget everything else, the whole world. Myself, above all. The "myself" that I flaunt every day.

'I don't...' I bite my lips and squint my eyes. I leave the tea, and I sit in front of Raymond. 'I can't even stand the idea of him with other women. With the girls that he could meet every day, anywhere. On the street, in a shop, in a pub. I can't even stand him having appointments with the clients anymore; I'm trying to avoid it, but...'

'Miranda, you must stop sending him away. Or the day will come when he'll stop coming back to you.' Raymond stands up, gets the cups of tea, and hands me mine. 'Try asking yourself if it's really what you want. But if you choose to give up this love, be careful. Because then you can also spend your life regretting it, but you will be forced to live with your choice.'

Julie

The single party. Miranda explained to me what it was about and involved me in the preparation. And since I'm single and I understand cooking (or at least I should understand it), I accepted enthusiastically to help her with the food. I really like the idea.

Meanwhile, a piece of news has spread in recent days. I'm not sure if it's real news or a rumour. It was Kara who informed me, but some of the guys also talked about it and seemed somewhat interested in the issue.

It seems that Stephen has started, for some time, being a professional cam boy. I'm not sure what it's about. Indeed, I know, I inquired. I don't know exactly how it works; that's it. I know, theoretically, that the guys do hardcore shows in front of the webcam. Then, they publish them on a site. And there are clients, mostly women I suppose to see the boys, who pay to watch them. Or they can also do live video, Kara explained to me.

'But did you see them? Have you seen Stephen? Does Miranda know?' I can't help but question her because I can't keep my curiosity.

'I think so, even if she pretends she doesn't, and she's certainly annoyed. But then, what could she do? She herself sells appointments with handsome guys to women. And in any case, she can't control everything that happens during and after the appointment. However, it seems that Michael is also moving into the same profession. And no, I haven't seen them... not yet.'

'Michael?' I can't help thinking about it. Michael lives with Giles, so that he will record his videos from there. This means that maybe even Giles...

'They can make a lot of money, apparently.'

'Oh, are you really sure?' I'm not convinced at all; I don't like the idea. But I'm curious, and I want to know more. Kara is also thrilled with the news and gives me all the details she knows.

Later in the day, as Stephen walks past us with his usual sexy and disarming smile, I'm almost tempted to ask him for more details. I barely control myself because it's elsewhere that I want to investigate from another source.

I have lunch with Giles in the city centre the following day. We meet at the Parnell Heritage Pub, one of Dublin's historic pubs. For a while, I decide to let go, not worry about anything, and enjoy the relaxing atmosphere of the place and his company.

Sitting on one of the sofas, I feel embraced by the warmth and the background music. Giles also seems to like this place.

Meanwhile, he tells me that he has been contacted for interviews by companies dealing with computer equipment. Maybe he wants to let me know he won't work for Miranda's agency for long. Unlike Stephen and Michael, it's just a temporary occupation for him.

'So, you're not going to undertake Stephen's new job? I heard that Michael started as well...'

I introduce the subject as purely coincidental and don't care much.

Giles sighs and shakes his head. But he doesn't answer my question directly. 'Miranda sent Michael away.'

'Do you think it was for that reason? I mean...' I don't even know what I mean. I realized the tension between them. And I also realized that it almost certainly depends on something else.

Giles doesn't reply but encourages me to continue. 'What do you think?'

'I don't know... has he broken the agency's rules? But at this point, Stephen too.' It's not really what I think. I expected him to continue the conversation. Obviously, the reasons are others. And I'm also trying to figure out if Giles will try the new work of Stephen and his cousin, which is apparently less demanding and more profitable. So, I keep clutching at straws. 'Maybe he goes out with other women outside his deals with Miranda. Do you know something? Do you know if Michael goes out with some other girl?'

'Miranda can't control everything and everyone. It's obvious that the boys see other women. Including Michael!' He answers me, almost annoyed by my question, so I look for an excuse to talk about something else, and I improvise a discussion about the most characteristic places in Dublin.

After lunch, we walk through most of O'Connell Street, and then we end up walking on Henry Street. It's a cold day, and I

143

wrap myself tight in my jacket, winding up my scarf around my neck. I was told that February is probably the coldest month in Ireland, often even worse than December and January. At this point, I'm forced to believe it.

'You... do you see other women?'

Inevitably, I pick up the previous conversation. I wanted to avoid it, but I couldn't. I don't even know where I want to bring my question because, as far as I know, Giles only had a date with Valerie.

'The only one I see at the moment outside the agency is you.' He replies immediately, without thinking about it too much. So, I don't think it's a calculated answer. He smiles and gives me an amused look. 'Even if maybe you meant something else with "seeing".'

'Yes, I meant something else.' I smile, look back at him, and then stare straight at him, embarrassed.

'And you?' He asks me, catching me off guard.

'I have no agreement with the agency', I reply diplomatically.

'So, you're free to go out with whoever you like?'

'Apparently not.'

We're wandering, maybe heading back to Parnell Street after walking around Jervis Street. I feel tired and a little frustrated. For too long now. And I don't even know who to talk to about my discomfort for not being able to achieve my goals. I do not even see a little progress, just to encourage me.

'Why not?'

He suddenly stops. I'm forced to stop, too, and turn to him. He frowns thoughtfully and squeezes his eyes.

'With whom would you like to "go out"? With Stephen, maybe? Or with one of the other guys? Maybe with Michael? Are you interested in Michael?'

Nice try, Giles, but I don't buy it! 'Even if I wanted it, they would be off limits to me, wouldn't they?'

'I suppose so...'

144

We continue walking in silence. I feel a growing tension in me between us. Along Henry Street, more or less in front of the Arnotts department store, a guy with a guitar is singing a love song. I recognize the tune first, then the words of *Something about the way you look tonight*.

"And I can't explain
But it's something about the way you look tonight
Takes my breath away
It's that feeling I get about you, deep inside..."

And the feeling of annoyance, of discomfort, still comes. Sudden, unexpected. Instead, I should expect it by now because it comes every time.

'Julie... Julie?'

Giles stops and looks at me. I'm staring at the young musician as if he was a ghost. Indeed, he is, maybe not directly. The ghost of a past love. That hurt me, making me feel useless and inadequate.

'This song...' I decide to confess; I don't want to invent an excuse that doesn't exist to try to hide the truth. 'I hate it, even if it's so beautiful. But my ex left me with this song in the background. And I...' I sigh deeply, and I look at him. 'I can't explain; at some point, I wasn't even listening to him anymore. It was as if I had put the mute button on in a movie; he was talking and talking... he was trying to explain why... why he didn't want me anymore. Why I wasn't good while someone else was. But I could only hear Elton John singing *Something about the way you look tonight...* and he was saying something completely different. But he, Philippe... he couldn't know or understand it.'

I realize I've said too much. I look down, trying to regain control of myself and my emotions, but the tears prick my eyes without pity on the situation I find myself in. In the middle of the street, among strangers who walk quickly and clash with my immobility, with my feeling of abandonment.

Suddenly, I feel tightened, my waist and my back caressed.

'Dance with me, Julie...' Giles put his arms around me, slowly whispering my name. I feel his breath on my temple, and for a moment, I close my eyes and let myself go.

Then I lift my face, and I look at him. His green eyes in mine, his lips so close. The agency's rules no longer exist, this place no longer exists, all these people on one of the busiest streets of the centre. And Philippe, his abandonment, no longer exists. But this song still exists in the background. And Giles, who is trying to comfort me, to console my malaise with the goodness of his heart.

'We can't...' I narrow my eyes to savour the feeling of his arms around me for a moment. But then, inevitably, I detach myself from him. 'Thank you, Giles. But we can't erase an emotion by overlapping it with another one.'

'I know we can't.' He gently strokes my arms before letting me go. 'That wasn't my intention.'

CHAPTER 24

Michael

'In your opinion, what is she thinking?'

Giles has been talking to me for an hour. About the story between him, Julie, and Valerie. One of the most senseless triangles that ever existed. And I'm enduring with passive patience.

'You believe that Julie may be interested in you, but in the meantime, she pushes you to see her friend Valerie.' I summarize the focus of the "problem". I have no desire to even deal with his dilemmas. I listen to him, trying to get mine off my mind. I listen to him because he's my cousin and we share the same apartment. And also, for not being the usual asshole who doesn't give a shit about anything and anyone.

'Yes... and I, like an idiot, am also trying to please her. I promised her to go out with Valerie again. And Valerie, but this Julie doesn't know, is aware of everything. So...'

'So, you're left without Julie and without Valerie. You're really a mess, a poor loser in short!'

I wonder why he doesn't decide to talk to the one he really wants. But maybe I understand him after all. I did it, and the results were disastrous!

'If Julie insists that I go out with her friend, that means...'

Here, he came to the conclusion by himself.

'Obvious. That she doesn't want you. This would be evident for human beings with average normal brains and attitudes. But we're talking about women!' Of some women, to be exact. I feel very male chauvinist now, but I don't give a damn.

'Not all situations reflect yours with Miranda', he replies with annoyance.

That's it, hit and sunk. But he's right. Inevitably, I tend to interpret the behaviour of all women holding Miranda Crossing as a "point of reference". Creepy, really!

'Maybe I should go out with Valerie.' I really don't want to talk about Miranda and extrapolate my hurt feelings. I prefer to change the subject. In fact, I'd rather even change the woman. Maybe Valerie could be for me, even just to have fun. 'At least I'd get rid of the problem and of Julie's fixation on setting you up with her friend. And you could make a move on her, at last. But I advise you not to wait too long. Women can be extremely complicated as well as fickle.'

Miranda

I knew this day would come again this year. Strangely, however, a week before Valentine's Day, not the same day. I confess that a part of me, for a moment, thought I could avoid it. But it's important to him. So, once again, I submissive accept, and I follow him without opposing, without questioning.

Now we are standing, staring down. I hold my arms very tightly along my body, my fingers crossed. I can't pray; I've never been able to do it easily. It has always been a commitment for me. I keep myself composed only because of the place and the situation. And I wait for Raymond to finish his silent prayers, meditations, or any thoughts, to finally leave the cold silence of the Glasnevin Cemetery and return home, not at the agency. At home, wrapped in a warm blanket to get rid of the melancholy with a cup of hot chocolate.

Suddenly, I realize that all kinds of people are buried at the Glasnevin Cemetery, united by a common destiny. Important, famous and powerful people as well as perfect strangers, poor and desperate. I sigh and look up for a moment to look around. I lose myself looking at the splendid decorations of the tombstones, with Celtic crosses, motifs with geometric designs, fantastic animals and flowers woven together. There's so much history here; you can breathe an atmosphere of magic mixed with sacredness. Everything seems intangible and perfect, far from reality and from the concerns that accompany our everyday lives.

After passing by the tomb of Paula, Raymond's wife, we find ourselves on that of my Aunt Grace. And on the headstone beyond her photograph, I reread the date. February 14th, the day she was born. Paula, on the other hand, died on February 12th. It is curious that two important women in a man's life were born and died a few days later in the same month.

'Suffering leads to distancing love.'

Raymond's statement seems aimed at the universe, not directly at me. So, I can even pretend to ignore it.

'Why are we here early this year?' I look at him. I've learned that everything in Raymond's behaviour has an explanation. Every gesture, every word.

'I tried to make room for some happiness this year. Not just for those I lost.'

He adds nothing more, and I don't ask. Maybe I understand, maybe I don't want to know. Or maybe I think it's better not to ask for confirmation. Paula and Grace, at different times, were the women of Raymond's life. Is there always room? Is there always time for another love? Not even this I want to know. I only know that I prefer not to take risks.

Back at Finglas, I take refuge at home, as I had decided. I leave Juliette and Kara at the agency. I wrap myself in the blanket on the couch. The sense of loneliness grips my soul more than ever. I spent most of my life in this city and have nobody,

149

really nobody but Raymond and some casual acquaintances. I realize how depressing it is. And that is the same for many, not just for me.

I glance at my cell phone, placed beside me. Before I even think clearly, I write a message and send it. The answer comes to me a few minutes later. Juliette replies that she would like to come over for dinner but has an appointment with Valerie.

'Invite her too. We'll order something good to eat and watch some movies.'

I answer instantly, feeling stupid this time. I seem like a little girl who begs her friends to spend the evening with her, to give her a chance, not to leave her alone. I look forward to Juliette's message.

'All right! I will arrive soon, and Valerie will join us.'

She also sends me a smiley face. So, a few hours later, I find myself sitting on the couch with Juliette and her friend Valerie. Each wrapped in a warm blanket, with leftovers of pizza, Chinese food, and tiramisu, as if we were lifelong friends. Watching old romantic comedies that we already know by heart but that heal the soul, especially staying warm in a cold winter.

'I'll never understand why she didn't choose William Holden in the end.' Juliette sighs and shakes her head, showing her disappointment as the credits roll across the screen.

'Yes, me too. I ask myself every time...' adds Valerie, rolling her eyes.

'Humphrey Bogart had more charisma, more personality...' I try to be the most reasonable. I also use the name of one of the two male actors instead of that of the movie's character *in Sabrina*, starring Audrey Hepburn. Before admitting what I have always thought too. 'Bullshit! Anyone would have chosen William Holden!'

'Trent turned up again.' Valerie's reply arrives unexpectedly and out of context. She shrugs and sighs, biting her lips. 'My ex...' She addresses me directly in case I have any doubts about it.

'What does he want? You are not thinking of going back with him, are you?' Juliette's almost horrified tone gradually rises.

'He probably remembered that he should have married me in a week.'

I follow their conversation without intruding. I already know the situation; Juliette told me everything when we met. Valerie's ex is the main reason she contacted the agency.

'He's an asshole, Val!' Juliette doesn't give up trying to discourage her friend. Her blue eyes seem to throw flames now; if she had Trent in front of her, she would incinerate him with her look. Valerie, in comparison, is much more serene and calm. 'Don't even think about it! That's why I made you go out with...'

'I don't know what I'll do with him. I only know I'll keep him on the edge for a while.' Valerie chuckles and pulls her knees to her chest. Juliette and I watch her. Only a woman who no longer feels anything towards a man can be so indifferent and determined towards him. In fact, Valerie adds something that confirms my hypothesis. 'After all, revenge is a dish best served cold. That's what they say, isn't it?'

She looks for an answer in me this time. I just have to nod and confirm.

'Yes, that's what they say. Theoretically, it should work and be simple, but...'

'I believe that when a person hurts us, very badly...' Valerie sometimes gets tangled up with words; her French accent makes her really tender and vulnerable at the same time. But she knows very well what she wants. Much more than I and Juliette put together. 'There is only one possible revenge that requires no effort on the part of the one who has suffered... happiness.'

CHAPTER 25

Giles

Julie's unjustified insistence almost forced me to go out again with Valerie. She explained to me that her ex had turned up again, so I had to stop her from the temptation of giving him another chance. However, Valerie doesn't seem to have the slightest intention.

Therefore, I find myself talking to Valerie about this and that, considering she now knows everything about me and the agency. She asks me how I ended up working for Miranda. I tell her the truth about Trasks and my dismissal. The one that, out of shame, I didn't dare to confess to Julie. So, I became a "St Valentine's Secret Agent" waiting for a better opportunity.

I meet Julie the following morning. She brings to my place Sarah's computer, the food blogger she works for as an assistant when she's not in the agency with Miranda. Apparently, she made a mess again by downloading files with a virus.

I don't understand her insistence on wanting to manage our lives, mine and her friend Valerie's, as if we were supposed to be together. My only hypothesis is that she's trying to distance me and make me understand that I have no hope with her. Maybe all the questions she asked me about the other guys, about Michael most of all, depend on this. Because Valerie is not suffering at all for her ex, she can find someone else if she wants. Without dragging tensions or unresolved suffering. But Julie... no, I just can't say the same about Julie; that's the problem. Maybe the same cannot be said about me either; this is the truth.

Basically, ironically, the person we are trying to help is the one who least needs our help.

'Do you think I would be more charming with foreign girls if I talked about being Irish or Scottish?' I try to provoke her even though I doubt I can get results this way. From the sentimental point of view, she's like an impregnable fortress most of the time. She even got worse when she heard that song on Grafton Street.

'I am a foreigner... and so is Val...' she frowns and wrinkles her nose in a way I now recognise, giving her a funny but sweet expression. So much so that I would like to kiss her now. 'And no, I guarantee you wouldn't be more charming, not at all!'

'Too bad, I was going to try in case Miranda set me up a real date with some client. Maybe in a day or two, she said she'll need me.'

'You don't really want to do that, do you?' Her expression has changed now. From funny to resentful.

'Why shouldn't I?' I shrug indifferently. 'I don't think I'm good at imitating the Scottish accent, but I can try.'

And I really try to give it a shot while I say the last sentence, without any success, I'm afraid.

'I didn't mean that!' She raises her voice, grabbing my arm and squeezing it almost tightly. When she realises it, she lets me go immediately. She sighs and nods briefly. 'I mean, I understand that... you accepted the job, so...'

'So sooner or later, it will happen. Sooner, I believe, it's Valentine's Day week, and Miranda must exploit me to the fullest. And besides your friend Valerie...' I decide that it's absurd to try to carry on this scene. By now, we all know it's just a facade. Only Julie doesn't know yet that there will never be anything that she would like to happen between me and Valerie. 'She's not interested in me, Julie. She's a beautiful girl, but I'm not interested in her either. So, we should end it here. Because...'

Julie sighs and closes her eyes for a moment. 'Do you know what the truth is, Giles?' She doesn't seem to have paid any attention to my talk about my relationship with Valerie. 'It hurts anyway. You hurt, you guys. It doesn't matter where you come from or what your accent is. When you leave, you hurt anyway.'

Julie

I could not interpret his look. Maybe I shouldn't have said what I said. He seemed resentful, almost angry. I didn't mean him, of course. And I don't know why I got him involved in the matter. Almost as if I feared him. In fact, it's true; I fear him. I listened to what he told me about Valerie, even though I pretended not to understand.

Because I know... because I feel... and I'm afraid to go further. This is not the right time. I'm not the right girl. And I still have that song that resonates in my head, which isn't even the soundtrack of Philippe's dry and cynical abandonment anymore. It's the soundtrack of my life. And Giles... could be yet my umpteenth failed attempt because they all have one thing in common, or almost. In the beginning, when they find me amazing. Okay, with Giles, it didn't happen that way; he didn't find me amazing. I don't think he finds me amazing even now. It's better this way.

My days have become intense between working as Sarah's assistant, three afternoons and two mornings at Miranda's agency and the cooking class three evenings a week. So much so that I almost have difficulty managing my moments' break.

It might be the tiredness or too many thoughts, but I can no longer follow the course as I should, even when there is Kate as a teacher. It could be tiredness, for sure, which affects my performance when we have practical tests. So, my mixed vegetables and sweet potato pie creation makes a poor end. It looks like an unattractive mush, so nobody would want to taste it even if it tasted pleasant.

'Not close to good enough, I'm afraid.' Kate approaches my table and looks from me to my poor, formless creature. 'Are you sure you really care?'

I don't understand what she is referring to. I look at her and feel myself sinking. Kate is charming, lively, dynamic and a highly respected professional in her environment and beyond. She travelled all over the world thanks to her work. She tilts her face while looking up at me. There is no comparison between us, even though we have the same eyes and hair colour. Blue eyes and brown hair, but she's an accomplished woman who has achieved everything in her life. I am... me.

'I'm sorry...' I find myself saying without understanding her words or fearing that I have understood them too well.

'I've been watching you for a while. There are so many jobs that could be more suitable for you.' She gives me a condescending smile and moves on to another table, leaving me alone to dispose of the disappointment and frustration triggered by her words. Words that, I realise, I understood very well.

I spend the following morning copying on the computer and fixing some of Sarah's articles with the related images attached. I'm tempted to ask her what she thinks of my work. Maybe I'm too tired and stressed by overwhelming thoughts to focus on what my real job will be.

I just have to get her at the right time, as soon as she returns. A moment in which she's not thinking about anything else, she's not engaged in a telephone conversation or, in any case, focused on her favourite topic: herself. Basically, I realise that Sarah will never have time for me, not even a few minutes, to calm me down. And I'm not entirely sure I really want to know her opinion. Especially since I fear she will confirm Kate's.

I leave Sarah's house as soon as she returns, and when she asks me if I can take care of the children, even if at short notice, I refuse without thinking about it too much. I don't want to make up an excuse. And I don't even care about needing her to launch my career, my real job, the job that doesn't even seem so real to me now. I just refuse; I'm tired of being exploited.

I find myself in my apartment in Rathmines. I feel useless and discouraged. And I'm starting to wonder what I'm really doing here. I invested too much in this place and job to let it all go. So, I do just what I shouldn't do. I call Giles. I don't even wonder why I called him, but he was the first one I thought of. I ask him to meet me if he can.

'Just enough time to leave my home, and I'll be there', he replies with a note of concern.

'Are you sure you have nothing else to do?' I reply hesitantly.

'I'm sure. Stay where you are. I'm coming.'

While I wait for him, I fall more and more into uncertainty. What if I really had it all wrong? I feel like a failure in all fields. I try to breathe regularly, but I feel a tightness in my chest that doesn't give me respite.

I find myself half an hour later sitting on the couch with Giles. In an uninterrupted flow of words, I told him everything that happened, first with Kate and then with Sarah. I'm so out of my mind that I even forgot good manners.

'Sorry... do you want something to drink? I'll make you some tea or...'

'No, Julie. I'm fine, don't worry,' he sighs and puts his hand on my shoulder. He slightly tilts his face to meet my eyes.

'The truth is, I don't know what to do. I'm afraid that...' I bite my lips and lower my head even more. 'I'm afraid Kate is right. And I don't know if I have enough will and motivation to contradict her.'

'Julie, listen to me... Do you know when everyone is telling someone that he will never be able to do something, in short, that he's really a failure in that field, he will never succeed, and he should change his job?'

I nod briefly and give him a puzzled look. I don't know what his point is. Basically, it's what Kate told me.

'Well, the someone I'm talking about will work hard to prove otherwise; he will fight to achieve his goals, and so everyone will realise that they were wrong. But Julie, are you... Are you really this "someone"? Is it really what you want to become, a food blogger or cooking expert? Because sometimes I feel that you're sticking to something you don't really want.'

I remain silent; I close my eyes and massage my forehead with my fingers. The truth? The truth is that I don't even know how to answer him.

So, I don't answer him, not directly. It would mean getting involved too much. In my last years, I have already invested in my chosen profession. 'I should attend more courses, that's it, in addition to working harder. My problem is that I'm not qualified enough, so Kate and Sarah scorn me. But the courses are expensive. If I improved my qualifications with Kate, I would immediately find a job in my field.'

'If that's the problem, I can help you.' Giles smiles and puts his hand on mine, which I hold onto my knees with my fingers intertwined. 'Finding money for your courses won't be so difficult.'

'No, Giles... no, absolutely not.' I blush with shame. I could never take money from him!

'It would only be a loan.' He doesn't give up and takes both my hands in his. 'As soon as you are an established food blogger, you can pay me back...'

'No, absolutely not, I said!' I withdraw my hands and pull away from him almost angrily.

When I look up, I read the disappointment in his eyes. Not so much for refusing his financial help but for my gesture.

'I'm sorry...' This time, I grab his hands and hold them in mine. 'I thank you with all my heart, Giles, really. But I would like to make it on my own...'

'It's okay', he smiles and nods, half closing his eyes and setting them on my face.

Unexpectedly, he caresses my hair gently, keeping his eyes gazing at mine. And I feel what is going to happen. I wouldn't want to. Indeed, I would like to avoid it. But a part of me can't resist; it doesn't want to resist anymore.

When he takes me in his arms and starts kissing me on my lips, I oppose with minimum resistance, which becomes ever more inconsistent. I let myself go. Because I can't do anything else. Because I don't want to do anything else. I'm tired. I'm tired of fighting, tired of keeping my distance. Above all, I'm tired of trying to avoid something I wanted from the first moment I laid my eyes on him.

CHAPTER 26

Miranda

Leaving my home and crossing the street, I find myself before her. Yes, just her who promises me love with her persuasive words since... since when? I don't remember. Maybe I don't even care. I find her, strangely, in front of the agency building. I wonder what she's doing here.

'Did you change your location?'

'No. I just came to see you more closely.' She opens her mouth wide with a smile and starts laughing, even if a little too loudly. It would be a beautiful smile if it weren't for the lack of most of her teeth.

'You certainly don't make a good deal, Tally. I don't have sweets with me, nothing to eat. If you want, I'll give you a few Euros to go and get something from the supermarket. But don't steal anything, okay? Sooner or later, they will get tired of letting you get away with it.'

'I don't steal! I've never stolen, I've never!' Now she points her undefined colour eyes at my face, more hurt than ever, and looks at me with an almost shocked expression. 'I was just looking at that box of chocolates, I was...'

Tally's accent is indefinable, a bit like the colour of her eyes. It's not typical of Finglas; it doesn't belong to any part of Ireland. Actually, it's very similar to mine. But I really believe that this small homeless woman tends to adopt the accent of anyone who speaks to her.

Suddenly, she shifts her gaze to the entrance of the building. And a suspicion sneaks into my mind, more and more insistently.

I'm not good at understanding these things. I'm not even good at interpreting feelings or reading people's hearts. But turning and following the direction of Tally's gaze, I no longer have any doubts. And I understand that the encouraging words she has always addressed me could be addressed to everyone. Herself included. Because the first to believe in them was always herself, Tally.

Julie

I can't believe it when I find them, among other requests that have arrived at the agency. And instinctively, I can't help but call Giles and ask him to meet me as soon as possible.

'No way! I can't believe it!'

'I thought exactly the same!' I reply, unable to stop laughing. I almost have tears in my eyes.

Because, among other clients' requests, I found Annette Trask's. Not just that, but even the one of her husband, Gerrit Trask, who evidently thought it was possible to make a request for men looking for a woman. He even threw in a physical description. He wants her tall, prosperous and with a great ass, possibly with long black hair.

'We can send him Miranda! So, she will tear him into pieces with just one look!' Giles continues laughing, stroking my back.

'Do you think Miranda has a great ass?' I cross my arms and give him a grim look. But then I can't stop myself, and I start laughing again. 'Maybe we both could show up! No thinking on, better not. I'm not sending you to Annette.'

'Gerrit Trask was so pissed off at me and the flyers, and then... here he is!' Giles smiles and shakes his head.

He told me about his "adventure" with Trask and his wife. He explained to me how and why he was fired. Last night, after the kiss, we spent the evening talking and clarifying. And kissing again.

'They both declare themselves single and willing to start a relationship!' I point my finger at the computer to show him the exact spot before the wife's request, then her husband's. Both have attached their photograph.

'We could let these two have a memorable joke.' Giles rubs his hands and gives me a sadistic look.

'What do you have in mind?'

'Soon you will know!' Giles laughs aloud, draws me to him and kisses me on my lips.

'Not even a little anticipation?' I have a vague idea of what Giles might be up to, but I would like confirmation.

'Can I organise it for them?'

'Don't get me in trouble with Miranda, though!'

'Don't worry... under the assumption that here they both declare themselves single and available and that Annette has used her maiden name, there will be no problem for you or the agency.'

CHAPTER 27

Michael

I saw her hurry up. I tried to reach her, but she had already taken the stairs. She didn't seem to want to avoid me because I don't think she noticed me. She evidently tried to ignore them.

To me, too, they have a somewhat strange effect, after all. Or rather, unexpected. Because, in fact, one of the last things in the world that I would have expected was to see that bizarre creature Tally in the arms of old Raymond.

'I see it's a good day, for you at least.' I can't help but stop and comment. I'm not even sarcastic for once.

'It will be for you too, dear', replies Tally promptly. Of course, everyone is happy for her; everyone will have a wonderful day, and everyone is in love and reciprocated. All are dear. This little woman still believes in fairy tales with a happy ending.

Raymond nods and smiles, stroking Tally's gaunt face.

'She's just gone upstairs. I'm sure she doesn't bite, but be careful.'

Obviously, I immediately understood who he was referring to, even if I hadn't seen her myself taking the stairs in a fury.

All I do is imitate her in this; I go past the reception and the desk, past Giles and Julie, barely greeting them. So, I enter her office without letting myself be announced and without knocking, opening the door with force.

She jolts and stares at me, almost horrified. Maybe also because I caught her in the act while she rummaged through that evil drawer.

'Don't you think the time has come to learn good manners?' She immediately recovers and stiffens, returning to her natural composure.

'Don't you think the time has come to throw out that fucking picture instead of continuing to cry over it?' I clumsily imitate her tone and her accent. And no way, dear Miranda. I really don't want to learn good manners. Not from you as a schoolteacher, above all. Because over the years, I've learned anything but it from you.

She gets up from her chair with a sudden movement that almost turns it upside down. She put both hands on the desk.

'Out.' She doesn't add anything else. She keeps an inexplicably low tone that is in stark contrast to the angry and horrified expression on her face.

I don't want it repeated twice. I turn and leave. Without adding anything else. Without trying to repair or rebuild. Because there is really nothing to repair, to rebuild. Absolutely nothing more. I will never come back. I will never see her again. And I will never again hold her in my arms and kiss her lips.

I exaggerated; I know. I realize it. I don't know how to handle my anger, my frustration when it comes to this woman. And to the bond she keeps with the man in the photo. So much so that she never gave me even a small space, the slightest chance.

And strangely, a song I had listened to as a kid echoes in my head. *One more try* by George Michael.

" 'Cause teacher
There are things that I don't want to learn
And the last one I had
Made me cry
So I know I don't want to learn to
Hold you, touch you
Think that you're mine
Because it ain't no joy
For an uptown boy

Whose teacher has told him goodbye, goodbye, goodbye."

Yes, she really was my "teacher". And now she's telling me goodbye. Forever.

Miranda

Someone knocks timidly at the door of my office. I doubt he came back. I would like it, though. I can't control myself. A part of me would like to hold him, kiss him. Another, which usually prevails, would like to slap him. I can't tolerate his vehemence. Although I am forced to admit it, it's one of his traits that most attracts me.

When I give her permission to enter, I find Juliette before me. Awkward and a bit weirded out. Passing in front of the desk she shares with Kara, I found her with Giles. I noticed a new harmony between them; maybe they finally clarified.

'Is it... all right?' Juliette almost doesn't dare speak to me, even though our relationship has changed after the evening spent at my house eating and watching movies.

'Sure.' I realize I have remained standing. I sit down and pick up some papers, without even knowing what it is, just to pretend I'm doing something.

She sighs deeply. I look at her well; she frowns, maybe trying to put together a catchphrase. In the end, what she manages to produce is rather disappointing.

'Michael has left.'

'Look at that! I noticed it, too. Maybe because, for a change, he was a villain, and I threw him out.'

'I'm sorry... Giles followed him.' She just whispers, clearly uneasy.

'Oh, you're sorry that Giles followed him and is no longer here laughing and joking with you.' I'm wicked, I know. I immediately take the chance that she serves me on a silver plate. But I can't help myself sometimes. Okay, often.

'No, it's not for that. Michael though...' She hesitates again. Do I have the power to terrorize everyone today? More than usual?

'Listen to me carefully, Juliette. I want to be clear. I run this agency because... it was left to me. I'm not even particularly inspired by this work, I know. I should have shut it down; I should have given up. There are so many things I should have done. But the truth is that my aunt and her friend founded it to consolidate their friendship and mutual support. They wanted to help other women find some company to feel less alone. Maybe a date could help. Raymond helped them and tracked down available men. Then, they spread the word, and it gradually became the agency it is now. My Aunt Grace, her friend Janet, and Raymond also belonged to a time when people still believed in romance and gallantry. Maybe in love as well. I never really believed in it. Maybe not even when I was married. I certainly won't start believing in it with a much younger guy who was just... an episode, let's say.'

More than an episode, he was a complete series of over ten seasons. But better not specify it.

'I'm sorry, then...' Here we go again. A contrite little face, a dejected look, and sad blue eyes. Juliette is of no support to me, indeed. 'For Michael, I'm sorry.'

Oh, here. It's better that she stressed well the subject of her displeasure. I open the drawer, grab the photograph, and throw it on the desk as if it were burning in my hands. Juliette comes closer and stretches towards me to look at it. My ex smiles at the camera, with his black eyes that simulate surprise and some expression line on his forehead. His light and well-combed hair contrasts his dark eyes and frames his face.

165

'My husband cheated on me with a girl who was half his age, almost. Despite the fact I'm not going to follow his example, what could I get from a guy like Michael? Also, considering that my ex-husband wasn't even as handsome and datable as he is.'

'So, you have the opinion that if an old, not really handsome man has abused you...' she stops, the continuation of the sentence is obvious.

I look at her, puzzled, and I only feel a great desire to laugh. If Carter, my ex, knew that a girl like Juliette called him an "old, not really handsome man", he would be shocked. With his self-esteem destroyed.

'No. But better not to risk it. I wouldn't be able to take the risk anymore. Michael has always hated the fact that I kept Carter's photo here, in the drawer. I've had it since he left me. Since I took over the management of the agency. It's the only one I have; I've thrown away all the others. I didn't even keep the wedding ones; I don't know what happened to them. I don't care. Michael believes I keep this picture here because I miss and love my ex-husband, and there is no hope for him. But the truth is that I often look at this photograph for one reason only... to remind myself not to fall again, to remember what happened to me, how much I suffered. Not because I still think of him. He stays in the drawer with my favourite chocolates; they help me move on. But it's not love; it's not a bond... It's just a reminder.'

CHAPTER 28

Julie

When Miranda told me her story, with that firm and determined but at the same time resigned tone, I didn't know what to say. How could I argue? I believe that Michael has sincere feelings for her, but... how can I not understand her? I'm sorry for Michael, but I can't help but sympathize with Miranda.

Maybe I've been too focused on myself lately. Because, in addition to the relationship between Miranda and Michael, another issue got out of hand. Valerie. Returning home in the evening, it was immediately clear why she was disinterested in Giles. I thought it was Trent's return. But no, he has another name. Stephen. I didn't catch them in intimate or compromising situations, but it was clear that there was something between them. Then Stephen left, and Valerie took refuge in her room. The excuse for Stephen's visit was to arrange some French lessons with Val.

I missed the details regarding their meeting and when they started seeing each other. Where, how, when?

I contact Stephen, and I almost force him to stop by the agency with the excuse of setting him up an appointment. I wait for him right behind the door. He realizes it immediately.

'All right, mademoiselle. Just tell me what you think.' He slightly widens his eyes at me in his incredibly sexy way. But that has no particular effect on me.

'Valerie will never accept the job you do', I sigh and go straight to the point without hesitating. 'I mean, not just this one... the other one as well, of which she knows nothing. That is always in the same area, in fact. Selling yourself.'

'Valerie knows it. Even about the other one that you don't mention. In any case, I'll give that up soon.' He stares at me again and bites his lips. 'I need it right now. My master's degree is costing me a lot. I know it's not a valid reason, and not everyone gets naked in front of a camera. There are other jobs, but...'

'Not everyone can afford to do it.' I shrug, and I give a look at his body. My intention is not to admire his physical attractiveness but to note a fact. 'I don't judge you, Stephen. You know, when I came here, I thought I would do the same. Not in front of a camera but in Miranda's agency. So, I'm not really in a position to make judgments. But Valerie, I don't want her to suffer and be disappointed again.'

'Julie...' He looks at me impatiently, or so I interpret it.

'All right! It's not my business; my friend has grown up enough to decide for herself.'

'No, actually, I was going to say it's lovely of you to protect her. But you don't have to worry about me. I'm not going to hurt her. And then... her ex does a very different job than mine, but that didn't stop him from betraying her and leaving her anyway. We had just met, and we decided to hang out. She knows what I do. I will stop shortly anyway. I have done it for money, you know.'

'Yes...' I know it very well. I know it so much that if I could, I would do it too, for money. So, I can't stop myself. I also feel a bit miserable and squalid because I called him to "scold him", and now I'm even considering asking him for information about it. 'Do you earn a lot by doing... what you do in front of the camera?'

Stephen frowns and looks at me, halfway amused and perplexed. 'Are you simply curious, or are you really interested?'

168

'Both things. No, actually, it's curiosity, but...' I sigh and shrug my shoulders. 'I just need to know how to get started, how I should be to do it. If you don't answer me, I'll look for information elsewhere. So, you better answer me, at least so I can avoid wasting time looking into the wrong sites.'

I need money, too. And what I can put together between Miranda's agency and Sarah's assistant job will never be enough. The rent is costing me too much. Everything is costing me too much. Valerie also doesn't earn much, but she already had money aside when she arrived here. Then, she is not spending a fortune on cooking classes taught by professionals in the field and by an internationally renowned chef.

'It's not that simple, Julie. It seems, maybe. But undressing in front of a camera can create serious problems. Sometimes, we also do live broadcasts with online viewers. Does Giles know you're looking for information about it?' He watches me suspiciously. He probably already knows about me and Giles.

'It's just between me and you. I need to make more money. I...' No, I wouldn't do it. Absolutely not. It was just a curiosity. Maybe a fantasy, like the idea of becoming a female "secret agent" in Miranda's agency. I decide to tell him everything, maybe Stephen could understand me. 'There are some cooking classes I would like to attend; I should. But I can't afford them. And I won't ask for help; I must get by myself and find a way.'

'I understand you.' Stephen nods and says nothing more.

From his eyes, I see he really understands me; he's not just saying it. I close my eyes for a moment; I feel exhausted. I already know, inside me, that I will never have the courage to do it. I'm just entertaining the idea; I'm just imagining.

'It's all simple for Giles. He doesn't really need it as much as I do. Even Miranda can't understand. Sometimes, it seems that some people get things just by wanting them. It never happens to me.'

'I understand what you mean, Julie. But the fact remains that you don't really want to do it.' His gaze now becomes stern, almost intransigent.

'Why, do you? Is there someone who would really like to do it?'

'Maybe... I never actually investigated.' Stephen shrugs and looks down. 'Don't act rashly, though. Think carefully. If you are really determined, I will help you.'

'Thank you, Stephen.' I smile and stroke his arm, then pull away from him.

Maybe he's one of the few who can understand me. But he's sceptical. Besides, so am I. It's just an idea, an attempt to explore an opportunity. I'll never really do it. Maybe I just want to find out if I can. Or try to understand if I have to start changing my perspective completely.

Giles

I don't even know if it's a good idea. I would like to prepare something special to make Julie understand that she must not fear that history will repeat itself. Not this time. Not with me, above all.

Meanwhile, I prepared the joke for the Trasks. There is not even a need to involve other people, actually. Miranda's agency doesn't accept male clients, but Gerrit probably didn't understand it. My diabolical plan is to schedule an appointment for them both in the same place. So, as soon as they find each other, they will have a lot of things to explain. As long as they don't run like hell, fearing the arrival of the infamous "St. Valentine's Secret Agent". I wonder which of the two will see the other one first.

Regarding Julie, I'm looking for Valerie's collaboration instead.

'As "St. Valentine's Secret Agents", don't you have anything already pre-packaged for the occasion?' She scans me attentively as if she already has suspicions about me.

Here is a strategic question. I'll have to confess that having missed the "mission" with her, Miranda has set me up a couple of appointments with an agency's client. Julie is still unaware of it, but sooner or later, she will find out. It's just a dinner and a walk along the river. And to follow whatever the client deems most appropriate. But no intimate relationship, of course.

'I think so. I haven't really started yet, so...' Exactly, not yet. Better not to say anything else. 'And then, you know by now, those are pre-packaged appointments in which nothing real happens.'

'Yes, I know. Julie knows it, too. However, as far as she's concerned, she still believes in this sort of "curse", so she's destined to always be alone on Valentine's Day. The truth is that even during the year, she has never had much luck.'

'This time, it won't be like that.' I reply firmly.

Valerie nods and smiles, even if a little doubtfully. 'Be careful. She tried to protect and comfort me after breaking up with my ex. But, the one who most needs protection and comfort is her.'

CHAPTER 29

Julie

I have no idea what Valerie meant by the words "I organized a little show'". Maybe because I can't think of anything very innocent after the conversation I had with Stephen in the afternoon.

In addition to inviting me, she also managed to convince Miranda, Giles and Stephen. She had asked Michael, too, but Miranda's presence automatically excluded his participation. I'm sorry they've got to this point. It could still be a good opportunity to clarify their feelings, although I'm afraid that by now, they have had too many without using even one.

We are sitting at a table in an Italian pizzeria on the Northside of the Liffey, one of the best in Dublin and the absolute favourite of mine and Valerie's. I can't believe my eyes when, about ten minutes later, I see Trent enter the front door. I'm afraid he's in the same condition as me because an incredulous expression is painted on his face. For a moment, at least. Because Valerie gets up and goes to welcome him with a happy and almost loving look, Trent recovers and holds her in his arms.

What the hell is going on? Miranda and Giles appear as confused as I am, but at least they maintain a confident composure. Stephen, however, seems perfectly at ease. I'm really missing something here.

Valerie and Trent are back, and he sits at the table with us. He takes his place at the head of the table next to Val. I still don't understand. Does she want to introduce Trent to the others?

Because as far as I'm concerned, I don't even want to remember that I know him already.

No, I don't believe it! Valerie can't be back with him after all he has put her through! At this point... here, looking at the situation, Stephen is much better!

I sigh and hold on to Giles' arm, sitting beside me. I don't even know if I'm looking for support from him or to use him as a release valve.

Suddenly, Trent himself breaks the silence, clearing his throat. I think he's going to introduce himself instead...

'I'm glad you agreed to see me here.' He smiles and takes the hand that Valerie holds on the table. 'I know it's your favourite restaurant in Dublin. And even if I thought I was going to meet you alone...'

'I asked you not to come and pick me up but to meet here instead because... I needed the support of my new friends. I didn't have any before... I mean, apart from Julie, of course.' Val speaks in a faint voice, almost as if she was moved. 'Before, I had only you, and maybe I was wrong not looking for anyone else, thinking that having only you was more than enough.'

When she names me, Valerie gives me a sweet look; her eyes are almost shiny. But I'm not, I'm not moved at all... and all I do is ask myself: what the hell is going on here? Because Trent seems just waiting for the right moment to do something I really wouldn't want to witness.

'Of course, I understand it. And you're right because I...'

Trent's voice becomes hoarse and deep. But of an annoying depth. His face turns red; he suddenly reminds me of one of those intermittent bulbs I had on a bedside lamp in my room as a child. The idea almost makes me laugh; I cover my mouth with my hand. I can seem surprised from the outside, but I'm just holding back a loud laugh. Another part of me would like to take him and throw him out of the window right behind the table. And push that silly friend of mine into Stephen's arms, who now lowers his face and sighs.

But damn it! Okay, he strips in front of a webcam, but he's much better than that asshole! Much better, from all points of view.

Trent now runs a hand through his blond hair with a wet look, as if it was wet with sweat. Valerie smiles at him expectantly, encouragingly. I would like to get up to go to the bathroom.

'I ask you again, Valerie. In front of your friends...' Trent touches his jacket, then he stops his hand at the pocket. I prefer to close my eyes when he takes out a little blue box and opens it. 'Valerie... will you marry me? I beg you to give me another chance because I love you. And nobody will ever love you as much as I do.'

When I decide to open them again, my eyes meet Miranda's. I try to communicate my unpleasant feelings and deep disapproval, and I would almost ask her to intervene, do something, or stop the whole scene. Instead, she quietly resumes watching the two protagonists, waiting for Valerie's reply.

'Trent, I... I really do believe it... in fact, I hope so...' Valerie seems so clumsy by forcing her French accent even more. Is she really moved? Her tone of voice is so sweet and suave. Trent seems to be eating out of her hand. 'I hope... nobody will ever love me as much as you do. Because you really loved me so horribly bad... like only a complete bastard could. You left me alone in this country after convincing me to move here for you; you made me feel lonely. So no, I'm not marrying you, and I won't tell you where you can shove your ring because I'm a polite person.'

Oh my God, I don't believe it! Not even Trent seems to believe it and remains staring at Valerie with a stupid expression because, despite the sense of her words, her tone of voice remains equally sweet and suave. And in the end, her accent is almost lost and improves considerably. Then I see her smile, turn to Stephen, and grab his hand. Giles, Miranda and I are surprised, but he's not. Because obviously, he knew.

Trent, without saying a word, gets up, picks up the little box and its contents, lowers his head, turns, and starts step by step towards the door. When he goes past it and exits, we all focus on Valerie. Stephen strokes her hair and pulls her to him to kiss her lips.

'Sorry for the little show. Now we can order and eat quietly if that's okay with you.' Valerie looks serene as if she has finally got a weight off her back.

The conversation resumes, and I remain silent. So, in the end, Val was not, has never been fragile and helpless as I have always believed. She has never been so in need of protection. I apologize and get up to go to the bathroom. I need a few minutes to recover.

'Julie...' As soon as I reach the bathroom, I find Valerie herself right behind me.

'Congratulations, Val. I wouldn't have been able to do the same.' However, I can't hide a note of resentment at not having made me part of her plan. 'Now I understand what you meant by that story of revenge that is best served cold. For sure, you have been able to take revenge well. Damn... not even the joke that Giles prepared for the Trasks can stand up to comparison. They just escaped from the restaurant as soon as they crossed paths, fearing the arrival of the "secret agents".' I keep talking about something else to say something and not letting Valerie understand how much I felt cut off from her life.

'Sorry if I didn't warn you, Julie. I wanted to keep the surprise effect. But with Stephen, I couldn't; you also understand why...'

'Yes, I understand.' I nod and smile; I decide to stop feeling hurt and embrace her with impetus. I'm happy for her. 'You did well.'

'I told you, I've let Trent go for a long time. But you didn't believe me. And apparently not even him.' Valerie sighs and shakes her head, suddenly looking worried. 'You, too, must

175

concentrate on the present, Julie. Giles really loves you; I see it. Try to be happy with him; give him a chance.'

'Yes, I will, Val. You're right; I'll let the past go. Because I'm falling in love with him too.'

Miranda

A few things still amaze me now. Valerie has succeeded. I wasn't entirely aware of becoming part of her little show staged against her cheating ex, but some suspicion had arisen in me. I realized that she was concocting something and that Stephen was part of the plan.

Those two are together, apparently. This means one thing, among the others. Stephen will soon abandon me: me and my agency. I'm already aware of his job in front of the webcam, even if I pretend nothing happened because he has always been a valid collaborator. I became very good at pretending nothing happened, it seems.

Juliette, however, the next day, still seems upset. Maybe she really believed Valerie intended to accept the asshole ex's proposal.

'Do you and Valerie still intend to help me with the singles party even though you are no longer single?' I ask her, stepping out of my office and stopping at her desk. No one is any more, apparently. Raymond also found a companion, betraying me and my party. The pseudo-engagements have spread like a plague epidemic in these recent days. Fortunately, I'm immune!

'Of course, I'm always available. And Val, too, I think.' She looks up at me; she smiles with her lips but is definitely thoughtful. 'Anyway, I'm not... hmm... so seriously involved, let's say.'

'You and Giles are good together.' I don't know what worries her, but I believe that in the coming days, after the damn Valentine's Day, I will have to make some fundamental decisions. And they also concern her. 'If you don't feel confident because of his job at the agency, don't worry. He's already looking for something else. And anyway, he's helping me with the computer maintenance because he's not excellent as a ladies' chaperone. In the last two appointments, he got away with it. He's nice, but the ladies don't crave to go out with him. He's obviously too busy with his real girlfriend and not very good at pretending with the others.'

'It's not for that, Miranda.' Juliette bites her lip and shakes her head briefly. 'There are too many unspoken things between Giles and me, too many unresolved issues. We don't know everything about each other. There are situations I can't deal with him. My situation with Giles is different from Valerie's with Stephen. I think it's much more like yours... with Michael.'

CHAPTER 30

Giles

Something wasn't working as it should have been. I had understood it. But I didn't expect her to go that far. Maybe, as Stephen says, it's just curiosity. In fact, it intrigued me, too. But in the end, I was under the illusion that we had clarified, that she had understood that she could count on me. After the problems in reaching her dream of becoming a food blogger, the joke about the Trasks and Valerie's "happy ending" story, I thought we had established a deeper bond between us.

No, it can't be. She won't actually do it. But then, why was Stephen so concerned about her? Why did she ask him to show her how to move in front of the webcam? She wanted to try, according to him. He advised me not to address her directly and to proceed calmly to try to understand her intentions. But also to stop her before she would regret it. Eventually, he realized that maybe he shouldn't have told me, but I preferred he did it.

I walk through the Ha'penny Bridge and continue to walk along the river on the other side of the city. The lights of the city are reflected on Liffey's water. It still gets dark relatively early, even though I'm confident that by the end of the month, the days will begin to lengthen and be less cold.

I need to talk to her. I must understand her reasons. It's like she's always rebelling against something, against someone. Against me as well, now. I had this impression from the beginning, from the first time I met her. Our relationship has just begun, but I feel she's slipping away from me, almost as if she wanted to wriggle away to take shelter, to stay safe. Coming to the point of leaving me, if necessary. As if she feared being rejected. And I must try to stop her before it's too late. Or rather, I must make sure she reacts, even if it means making her hate me.

Julie

I can't answer his question. Or maybe I don't want to. But yes, I want to. Because at least one way or another, it will be over.

'You don't want to really do it, do you?' Giles is clearly angry. He may have only known about it from Stephen because I haven't talked to anyone else. Above all, I told no one else I wanted to try.

'Yes, instead. I decided to do it as soon as possible. I need it and don't intend to ask for your permission.'

I'm not convinced at all that I want to do it. I don't know anything anymore. Really anything. It's as if my whole world had suddenly collapsed. Not suddenly, actually. It has been a stalemate for some time now, as if I was balanced on a wire without knowing which way to fall. But certain of having to fall, which in any case will be inevitable.

Giles gazes at me. He no longer seems angry for having kept my intentions hidden from him. Not even irritated by my statement or nervous. He just looks sad. But then we just met; he can't stake claims upon me.

'Then we have nothing more to say. You're not the one I thought; I made a big mistake with you.' He goes past the living room and heads straight for the front door without turning to look at me. Not even one last time.

'You're an asshole. And a chauvinist.' I should have said it a moment ago instead of waiting for him to be out the door.

But no, I'm not running after him. I won't stop him. I'll let him go. I wanted to argue with him, not that everything was going on in a calm, flat... balanced way. Even the bad words I addressed him were calm, flat, and balanced. It hurts more like this. And I don't know how to handle this pain that lurks inside and cannot even explode or find a voice of its own. He left, and he left me without arguing. Here, exactly... as if I wasn't even worth a discussion.

Everything I have fought for is leaving, not just Giles. My present, my past and even my future. The truth, which I've been fighting against for days, is that Kate and Sarah are right. I really don't understand anything about cooking. I never understood anything. In addition to not knowing how to cook, I can't even give an assessment on food as an expert or a professional. I threw away months and years without understanding anything or experiencing a real passion for what I was doing. I chose it because... only because it seemed like a good idea, an excellent source of income.

He left. Because I want to try a job that will make me feel uncomfortable, where I will earn money, I will need to pay for courses that will help me find another job I don't care about. What a fantastic plan! Almost brilliant, indeed! Yet everything fit perfectly before.

It's not just about Valentine's Day. Not even about the previous days. Even less about a song that always comes to my mind in the most complicated moments, like an alarm bell. Like a soundtrack that marks the fundamental passages of a movie or a television series. It always hurts. Being left always hurts at any time of the year.

I knew exactly what I meant when I told Miranda that my relationship with Giles was much like hers with Michael. She has that picture in the drawer, and I have the song in the background. It's not about our relationships; it's about us.

Miranda and I, in a sense, are the same; we have experienced the same condition.

And Giles needs to know. I wish he understood. That hurts me. I don't want to be a cam girl. I don't even care about becoming an important food blogger. He had understood it for a long time, a long time before me. So now he must know. I must tell him. No matter how and when, because being left by someone you love always hurts like hell. He hurt me like hell, too.

CHAPTER 31

Michael

She looked distraught. Indeed, I believe I haven't seen anyone so terrified. Not even me as a child. Yet I was never a very quiet type, and they almost had to tie me up in the dentist's chair because I bit him regularly at every visit.

Stephen and I accompanied Tally to the university's dental clinic. They have treated and implanted her new teeth, even if it will take some time before she gets used to having them again and can use them to eat naturally.

I knew I could get good conditions for her.

'Now I can eat all the chocolate I want!' She exclaims as soon as I take her back to Raymond's house. 'Not immediately, I understand. In a little while.'

I nod and give her a slight smile. I'm happy for Tally, but I can't express my enthusiasm. Especially in this place. So close to that cruel woman who took all of me, annihilating my self-esteem and dignity. I must try to forget her forever and strive to remove Miranda Crossing from my mind.

I cast a fleeting glance towards the stairs leading to the upper floor, that of the agency. I'm tempted, but I resist. I turn to leave. I could have asked Stephen to accompany Tally. But the truth is that, despite my efforts, I can't stay away from here.

I close my eyes for a moment. I must leave quickly. But when I open them again, I see her right in front of me, holding a supermarket bag.

We remain silent, as if we didn't know what to say. Or if it's appropriate to say something. I move sideways to let her pass and nod to greet her almost inaudibly. She does the same. I realize only now that, along with Miranda, Julie is also there.

'It's very nice what you did for Tally.' Unexpectedly, when I've already passed her and am about to open the glass door, her words reach me. She then clears her throat and seems to hesitate. 'Raymond told me...'

'Yes, you have been fantastic!' Julie confirms, and she is definitely more enthusiastic. Then, maybe embarrassed, she leaves us alone, almost rushing to the stairs.

Miranda stands still for a moment before following her much more slowly. I could take the opportunity to talk to her, but I don't know what to say. Because there is really nothing left, there are no more words to add between us.

'I would have done it for anyone.' So, I say the first thing that comes to my mind just not to remain silent. Although maybe I could have done better.

I'm leaving feeling a sense of liberation and despair at the same time. I'm leaving feeling shaky like I'm not perfectly stable on my legs. As if I had a hangover, that's it. And now I need time to recover, but without knowing exactly how much. Maybe a single day, maybe an eternity.

Miranda

'You fucked it up, admit it!' For sure, Juliette and I couldn't be more skilled at knowing how to ruin our love life. At least hers is a love life; mine will never find a proper definition.

'And what about you?' She replies in kind and gives me a reproaching look. Our relationship has considerably changed in the last few days, so much so that she tells me exactly what she thinks without being intimidated. 'You had Michael in front of

183

you, damn it! I ran ahead on purpose to leave you two alone, and what did you do? Nothing!'

'I tried to... I mean, I tried a little conversation.' I shake my head; I don't want to talk about myself. Specifically, I don't want to talk about me and Michael. 'Anyway, you asking Stephen for information on how to become a cam girl? You knew very well that he would tell Giles. It almost seems like you intentionally did it to destroy your relationship.'

'Actually, I didn't do anything. It was him. Evidently, it wasn't meant to be; if he can't understand me, he can't be with me.' Juliette scans me carefully, then snorts and leans with both hands at her desk. 'Giles and I have come to know each other recently. Things between you and Michael have been going on for years. Isn't it bullshit to be so in love with someone like you are with Michael and let him go? So don't come and preach me, then!'

Apparently, the best defence is the attack. So, Juliette continues to attack me for not responding and not taking responsibility. I take refuge in my office to avoid returning to the conversation about Michael and me.

If Juliette knew... I didn't let him go. I didn't let him go at all. Far from it! He's more than ever part of myself, my thoughts, and my life. Of my heart, above all. And I don't know what to do anymore, what to invent to tear him away.

CHAPTER 32

Julie

Evidently, Valerie and I could be the worthy protagonists of the soap opera "The Exes' Return". When I see an e-mail from Philippe, I can hardly believe it. I hadn't heard from him for more than a year. And even in his answers, there was always something distant, impersonal. Maybe because I was the one who encouraged them, he wrote to me because I needed an explanation from him. I wanted to understand. What was wrong with me? What was so wrong with me for him to leave me? Actually, I only made myself look ridiculous without even realizing it at the time.

I re-read his message. It's so different from the others that it looks like it has been sent to me by another person. I check his address, almost convinced that this must be a mistake. But it's not; it's really him unless someone has taken possession of his password as well as his e-mail address and is now having fun mocking me.

No, it's really him, apparently. I reply briefly, and he surprises me even more by writing back a few minutes later. He says he's in Dublin and he wants to meet me.

I'm not convinced at all. I don't understand what he's doing in Dublin. He has always been sceptical about visiting other countries, especially if they speak another language. Sceptical and very lazy as well. I doubt he's here for me.

I keep re-reading his message and take time to think about what to do. I don't really want to see him right now, during this time. But at the same time, I'm also curious. Besides, if I don't agree to meet him, he might think I'm still mad at him and hurt by what he did to me. Partly, that is true, but I don't want him to have confirmation of it.

I agree to see him in the centre the next day in the late morning. I never know what meeting point to indicate when I must meet someone. So, as always, I suggest the Eason bookstore's coffee shop on O'Connell Street. It should be easy to find, even for those who have just arrived in town.

In the evening, I obviously avoid telling Valerie. I don't even tell her that I received an e-mail from Philippe and that he is in town. I don't want to suffer her reproaches, even if they would be an exact copy of what I did with her regarding Trent. I don't care about Philippe anymore. I just want to know why he's in Dublin, and he looked for me.

'I've decided to give it a try.' That's Philippe's explanation, would you believe, the following day. While he scans me carefully with his dark eyes and the tuft of hair, he skilfully moves away from his face. A gesture that I had found fascinating and had won me over. Now, it seems almost annoying to me.

'So, from just one day to the other, you decided to leave for Dublin?' I feel uncomfortable as I stir my cappuccino, and looking at the pieces of torn paper around the cup, I'm afraid I put too many sugar sachets in it.

'More or less. I was also tempted by other cities, but in the end, I decided on Dublin.'

He sips his coffee and then looks back at me with a look I can't interpret. On the contrary, I'm afraid I can interpret it too well. But I simply just wouldn't want to give him that impression. Of one who hopes he has chosen, among many, precisely the city where she lives because she still has illusions towards him. I hate myself right now. I can't say anything intelligent and sensible that will permanently cancel his opinion about me. And I hate him, too. The self-confidence he has always shown, and that makes me feel fragile and vulnerable.

Inevitably, I really wonder if he's here for me. I don't want to know. I only know that I will let him go after this meeting. I won't ask him anything unless he wants to keep in contact with me. I'll let him go. But really, this time. Besides, I've become good at letting go. Our relationship has never been meaningful, at least for him. Now that he is sitting right in front of me, and everything between us could still change, I am absolutely certain that it's not for me either. Not anymore. Finally.

Miranda

Juliette spent the last half hour telling me about the return of her ex, Philippe. She has the satisfied expression of someone who has overcome it. She no longer cares about him, and now she's really convinced.

'Unfortunately, I didn't get the chance of an Oscar-winning scene like Valerie's with Trent. Philippe is too clever. Or I'm not like Valerie. However, I'm already happy enough to have freed my mind from his cumbersome presence, once and for all!'

'So, you mean that now you will finally have room for Giles?' My question arises spontaneously, but Juliette frowns as if I had ruined her "party".

I think she will avoid answering, but she surprises me. 'With Giles, the issue is another one. Until he realizes that I'm not his property and I take my own decisions alone... we will never get along.'

'I doubt a man could ever understand such a delicate concept!' I laugh and shake my head. 'Jokes aside, Giles is an understanding guy. You're the one who may be exaggerated a bit, Juliette. I don't think he's the type who considers you his property without respecting your wishes.'

Unlike Michael. I avoided saying it out loud because I would allow Juliette to reverse the discussion on me. And I also avoid revealing that the first thought after her tale of the ex's return immediately went to mine. My ex-husband. If he came back after Trent and Philippe, I could also believe in a really sneaky twist of fate. But I know that Carter won't come back. I know him. After trying miserably to rebuild our relationship, he left me with the full conviction of leaving me, without doubts, without second thoughts. Also, thanks to my silence war. He left me for another woman. Younger, more lively, more enthusiastic about life. Here, precisely, these were the words he used: "enthusiastic about life". Which I'm no longer. Or maybe, being born and raised sceptical and cynical, I've never been.

CHAPTER 33

Giles

So, Julie's infamous ex is back. Indeed, rather than being back, he showed up right here in Dublin. Maybe with claims towards her. I don't want to think about it. I came to know everything from others, not from her. Miranda has recommended that I do something to avoid losing her. That means she believes she can really go back with him. Otherwise, she wouldn't have said that. I honestly don't want to think about it.

'I can't even figure out for what absurd reason you broke up!' Valerie called my home with Stephen. She also seems seriously worried, just like Miranda. She believes that Philippe is a threat. But he's not. He can't be a threat to an already finished relationship. 'Don't tell me it's because of that nonsense that made her mind to become a cam girl! Julie would never do it; she's not the type!'

'Oh, so would I be the type?' Stephen scolds her, winks at her, and pinches her side.

'You will have to stop immediately; otherwise, I will intervene online among your spectators... clients... whatever they are called, in short... declaring "He's mine, hands down!!!!"'

Stephen bursts out laughing, and I smile too. They're good together despite their differences. They are so good that I almost feel envious of them.

Valerie sighs and becomes immediately serious, turning to me. 'Do your best, though. Don't leave her to Philippe. In any case, I don't think she'll get back to him. She's not crazy up to that point. Really, you shouldn't have broken up.'

'Julie doesn't want to accept my help, that's the main reason. And it was her who left me. Besides, she doesn't even talk to me anymore; her ex is back, and I heard it from Miranda!'

I would like to end the conversation once and for all. And while I'm at it, I would almost like to push Valerie, Stephen and their happiness out of my house. In this case, I prefer Michael; at least I can find some kind of solidarity on his part. As long as solidarity can be defined as wandering around the house constantly being sullen or tearing your hair out.

I'm adjusting to the slow passing of time, of days. Strangely, the hours seem endless lately. I decided to tell Miranda that I would no longer work for her as a "Secret Agent". Even if she already knew it from the start. But maybe now, after a few not-very-exciting appointments, we have both understood that it's better to let it go. I received some offers from the companies to which I had sent my CV, and some of them would like to set up some interviews. In the coming days, I will carefully evaluate them. The truth is that I'm no longer even sure I want to stay in this city.

I find myself in the agency, almost hoping to meet her. Even if a part of me would prefer not to see her at all. Not even Miranda is here. Kara asks me to wait for her; she should arrive soon.

I decide to go for a walk; I feel like an idiot. And I also feel lost in this area of Dublin. Indeed, throughout this country, I get that feeling. I'm reminded of my promise to my grandfather; maybe I should try to take it seriously. I could take the opportunity to do some exploratory tours and try to raise my spirits, away from here and from the temptation to look for Julie. Perhaps starting in Cork and Limerick, the two cities where my grandfather's family lived. I'm confident I will undoubtedly be able to find someone again.

I hear footsteps behind me. They're slightly heavy, shuffling steps. Turning around, I see Raymond. I don't know why he's following me to the corner coffee shop. I barely greet him, and then I turn around, intending to resume my way.

'Don't retreat; fight for your girlfriend.'

That's it, that's the last thing I need, him as well. Why does almost everyone have a great desire to give me advice that I have no intention of following? What would Raymond know about it?

I'd rather not answer and ignore him, pretending I didn't understand.

'It would be useless. It was useless even before. Raymond, fighting for someone who doesn't want to be there and prefers to stay away, is useless. It was like that in New York as well.' Maybe, starting from the idea of almost ignoring him, I said too much. I would like to rewind the tape and take back everything, but now it's too late. I went too far, and I'm sure Raymond will take advantage of it.

'Here in Dublin and with this girl, it might not be useless as it was in New York.' His voice comes to me again from behind but farther away. He has stopped, in fact. He's not following me anymore. 'Think well before giving up. In many years, you may regret not having fought. But you won't be able to go back.'

Julie

I don't know why I accepted his dinner invitation. I acted instinctively. I don't have much confidence in him because he always seems angry with the world, unlike the other guys who hang out in the agency, who are mostly funny and friendly. Angry with Miranda, actually. And he no longer hangs out in the agency; I would say he's avoiding it like the plague. So, I don't think his offer to go out for dinner depends on that or some strange request since he no longer works for Miranda. Despite everything, he's still an employee but certainly wouldn't go out with me as a "St. Valentine's Secret Agent". Indeed, he's the last person I would have expected to spend the eve of that day, the day that always brought me diabolically bad luck.

'So... did you invite me so I wouldn't be alone? Only out of pity for me? Or did someone ask you? You can be honest with me, Michael. If it's out of pity, I won't get offended, don't worry.'

'Giles didn't ask me if that's what you think. And not even your friend Valerie. It was my idea. And it's not even out of pity.'

He looks at me as if he wants to see inside my thoughts. There is a third option besides Giles and Valerie, which he didn't consider. Maybe he didn't consider it because it's just the one that prompted him to ask me out, so he's trying to keep it hidden as much as possible. He might want news about Miranda and believes he can get it from me. He saw us together, and he probably thinks I became a kind of friend and confidant of Miranda.

'Thank you, then.'

'I'm glad to be with you.' He nods and tries to smile. But it is a forced smile, tired, almost depressed. One thing is sure about Michael. He can't pretend, not even committing himself. In this, he's almost worse than Giles. It must have been highly complicated for him to work for the agency and spend time with women he doesn't care about.

We set off for a restaurant he knows in Temple Bar Square, which he told me about in his invitation message.

'Michael... I won't tell you anything about Miranda.' I decide to make things clear right away because I know that it wasn't his interest in me that made him ask me out. 'So don't try, that's it.'

'It's not to know about Miranda that I invited you to dinner. I know she's a lost cause for me by now.' He widens his green eyes at me, almost offended by my guess. 'But actually... even though he didn't ask me, it's for Giles that I wanted to see you and talk to you. Give him a chance. He hasn't had an easy time lately. Neither here nor when he was in New York. I can tell you if you want, even if he will be pissed off when he finds out. So... now that you know the real reason for my invitation, you can decide whether to have dinner with me or go home.'

He catches me off guard, and I could seriously part company with him and let him off down the river, turn around, and hole up at home to enjoy a romantic comedy. Indeed, maybe a thriller is better. But I can't. I really want to know. I want to hear about him. I don't know everything yet... and I suspect it's a lot.

'I have to eat anyway', I snort and roll my eyes, pretending to be offended. Then I sigh, and for a moment, I lose myself looking at the city lights reflected in the Liffey's water that flows quietly under its bridges. 'Anyway, about Miranda... she's not a lost cause.'

CHAPTER 34

Michael

I didn't lie to Julie. I really wanted her to know the truth about Giles before she unjustly condemned him. The way he was betrayed by his ex in New York and the problems with his father and grandfather. Being raised between them and their mutual hostility was complicated. Choosing to come to Ireland following his grandfather's suggestion made the relations with his father even more problematic.

But when she mentioned Miranda, I couldn't help but think of her again. Actually, I didn't need Julie to mention her. I'm always thinking about her, anyway. Day and night. I can't get her out of my head.

It was ridiculous to spend the evening before Valentine's Day with the girl who is currently closest to Miranda. Who is also my cousin's ex-girlfriend, despite having been together only a few days. This world is all wrong. This life is all wrong, as well as being unfairly complicated. Why do people never manage to have normal connections and relationships?

So, after greeting Julie and walking her home, instead of retiring to spend a sleepless night in my apartment on Parnell Street, I follow my instinct, and from O'Connell Street, I catch the 140 bus in the direction of Finglas. I hadn't planned it, but the bus arrived by chance just when I was at that point on the road, a few steps from the bus stop. I couldn't keep myself, couldn't avoid it.

At the Finglas Village stop, I walked the distance that separated me from her, and I found myself in front of her house while the light rain began to fall, wetting the asphalt little by little until it formed small puddles. I couldn't even knock on her door, but I remained like an idiot staring at it. Waiting for something I knew wouldn't have happened. Waiting for her to notice me.

I don't even know how much time has passed. I'm still here. I won't move. I keep waiting. The rain may mitigate the bitter cold of the last few days.

When I decide to leave, I find it hard to move. It almost feels like my feet have planted roots in the ground. I wonder what she's doing now, behind that door, behind her bedroom window. I wonder if the thought of me touches her, even for a moment. Maybe she'll be sleeping. Or maybe she saw me and decided not to open the door for me.

In any case, I'm leaving. I won't wait for a night bus that will never arrive. I decide to walk to the centre, no matter how long it takes. I need to walk to shake off this madness from me. The longing for her. The pain that she impressed on me like a brand. She refuses me. She doesn't want me. She doesn't believe me because she has learned the hard way not to trust anyone. I can't even blame her, after all. I also learned the hard way. And, what's worse, I learned from her.

Julie

I've been collecting dates lately. I have had more in these last days than during my whole existence.

Last night, Michael's unexpected dinner invitation, and this afternoon, just on Valentine's Day, an appointment with Philippe, who urgently needs to talk to me. Although I have no urgency towards him, I agree to see him. He asks me to meet at my house, but I refuse with the excuse of being at work at

195

Sarah's house in the morning and having to go to my second job right after lunch. Miranda's agency, even though I didn't mention it explicitly. Both are excuses. I asked Philippe to meet at lunch break, but the truth is I only have to go to Miranda in the late afternoon.

I already feel uncomfortable even before meeting him. A part of me rebels and feels strongly annoyed. Obviously, I didn't ask for advice. I know Valerie would have told me to tell him to go to hell. It's the same advice that I would give to myself. Like Alice in Wonderland, I'm good at giving myself great advice. Great advice, but I hardly ever follow them. I guess it's the same for most people. In one way or another, we are all a bit like Alice.

So, I gave Philippe an appointment at the Jervis Shopping Centre. I couldn't choose a more crowded location. As I'm tiredly walking there, I can't help thinking that it's right next to the place of my first meeting with Giles, the Trasks' electrical equipment store. I remember the scene perfectly, with Sarah's possessed children in tow. The leaflets of the agency "Secret Agents at Your Service" and all that followed. My crazy decision to find out more, the appointment with Miranda... and the following days. It all happened after my first meeting with Giles. It's strange sometimes how "life happens". Often, while people are busy making other plans. This is what happened to me.

This reminds me a little of what they call "the butterfly effect". The slightest whiff of a butterfly can cause a hurricane on the other side of the world. For me, no hurricane, of course. But in the meantime, after my chance meeting/clashing at the Trasks' shop, Valerie got together with Stephen and completely and rightly forgot about Trent. I... not, really. For me, no hurricane. Maybe I fell in love once again with the umpteenth wrong guy. Maybe I just have a crazy fear of suffering again. However...

However, I find Philippe at the main entrance of the Jervis Shopping Centre. And, overwhelmed by my thoughts, I totally forgot about him!

'Julie...'

He approaches me with a slightly forced smile. He looks uncomfortable as if he finds himself in an environment that doesn't belong to him, still hostile. I can understand the feeling.

'Hi, Philippe.'

He tries to hug me and kiss me. I return while maintaining a certain distance. I'm pretty sure that my lack of enthusiasm is tangible.

'Should we... stay here?' He has a sceptical expression; he seems to like the idea very little.

But I don't care; I won't please him or make things simpler for him. That time has gone.

'If you don't mind. I should eat something quickly before going to work.' I'm inflexible and distant. I realise that. I also realise I have the typical nonchalance of those who have settled in the new city despite the initial difficulties.

It doesn't really concern me. At the cost of taking the bus and going to Miranda far ahead of time, I'll follow my plan word for word. Whatever Philippe wants from me, I won't give him my time, my whole afternoon. I'd rather go and help Miranda with the singles party, even if it's still early.

'All right then. You decide the place you prefer.'

He's evidently unhappy and dissatisfied with my lack of openness. But he doesn't complain; he tries to smile as he strokes my back to guide me inside the shopping centre. I know him enough. He doesn't like this situation; it bothers him. But I don't care at all about how I make him feel.

I choose an ordinary self-service, medium crowded. We order, collect our trays, and sit between two students and a mother with three children at a free table. I start eating heartily while Philippe watches me, serious and composed. Maybe a bit too much.

'Julie, I... what I wanted to tell you...'

'Hmm...' I encourage him to continue while I chew my sandwich.

'I've decided to move here. Maybe I didn't tell you everything, but... I found a job, that's why I'm in Dublin. Now I have decided to accept the offer, but...'

Philippe in France worked for a telephone company. I don't know what kind of work he found. I don't ask. I let him speak. I just nod and give him a fake smile.

'I mean, I... I'm sorry about how things ended up between us.'

Now, he gives me a helpless and sad puppy look, typical of his dark eyes and way of doing things when he wants to get something from me. So, we moved on to a personal level from the conversation regarding his job.

'It was the right thing', I simply answer with a shrug. And the truth is that I'm more than ever convinced about it.

'No, it wasn't!' He doesn't let the chance slip away and responds in kind. Raising his voice a bit to overpower the shrill of the children sitting on one side and the laughter of the two students on the other. 'Julie, I realised I was wrong with you. Especially because... it didn't have to end this way. It didn't have to end at all. I ask you to forgive me, to give me another chance now that I'm here. And the fact that coincidently today is...'

Coincidently, today what? Is it Valentine's Day? And then?

'Philippe, if I have to be honest...' I interrupt him before giving him a chance to continue. No, I'm not like Valerie. I won't let him finish and then mock him or insult him. I'm not that cold; I can't. Or I'm not a great revenge strategist. Maybe because I'm too tired. I'm too tired to listen to him, see him, and have him in front of me with his pathetic and absurd excuses. 'I think it as well shouldn't have ended that way. It didn't have to end with you dumping me in the car, with a beautiful background song that made me suffer every time... because every time I happened to hear it again, I connected it to that moment. To you who dumped me in the car in the middle of nowhere without even giving me a chance to run away. To you who left me for someone else. But what do you know about it? You didn't listen to that song. You didn't even listen to me. You just listened to yourself. And even now... I have the feeling that you're just listening to yourself. Now that you're here, what changes? Do you feel lonely? Do you need help finding your way around the new city? I know the feeling; I know it too well. And if you want my forgiveness, you have it... I forgive you. But I will give another chance to someone who certainly deserves it more than you do.'

He stares at me in disbelief. He seems left speechless. Maybe it's because he really doesn't have other words to say. He doesn't know how to reply. I believe that, in the end, he doesn't even recognise me anymore.

'Regarding Valentine's Day...' I get up and pick up my tray and the remains of my lunch, ready to throw everything in the appropriate containers. Ready to throw Philippe, too, if possible. 'Valentine's Day was approaching even a year ago. But you didn't care at all. Now, instead, it seems, it suits you to remember it.'

CHAPTER 35

Giles

'I think she still cares. Try to recover, damn it! I understand you got mad about that cam girl bullshit, but it really seems absurd. It's obvious that she would never do it... everybody has bullshit like that crossing their mind occasionally.'

I don't know what happened to Michael. I met him in the morning, and he's been reduced to a wet rag or worse. His eyes are marked, and he looks like he has a slight fever. I don't think I've ever seen him look so poorly. So, the last thing he should be thinking of is to try to save the relationship between me and Julie.

'You know her ex is back, right?' I try to stop the conversation immediately and categorically. I'm getting ready to go out and don't want to waste time on sterile arguments. 'By now, she would already be back with him. So, let's end it here, Michael, please.'

'But she didn't go back with him, damn it! She won't go back with him! I saw her last night, I know it. It's you that she wants, don't be an asshole!' Michael's words are interspersed with repeated coughing. He passes a hand over his forehead. 'Shit!'

'You... did you see Julie last night?' Maybe I should worry more about his health, but Michael's revelation takes precedence over everything else. He included.

'Yes! We went out for dinner. And I don't give a damn if you get pissed off! She wants you back, so go get her, don't be a dick!'

'Oh God, what an asshole you are...' I shake my head in annoyance; I could punch him. But in the condition he is in at the moment, I would knock him out by only blowing on him. 'What the hell did you do? You look like...'

'Like someone who spent the night in the cold and in the rain staring at the door of a...' He bites his lips; evidently, he can't find the proper term to define her, but I understand who he's talking about. It's not so difficult to get there.

'And didn't it occur to you to knock and ask her to let you in? Or did she kick you out? But I doubt it...' No, she wouldn't have. Miranda is even more stubborn than he is, but she wouldn't have left him out all night.

'No. I didn't ask her to let me in. I didn't ask her anything this time. I don't think she even saw me; it was already past midnight when I arrived.'

I shake my head and sigh. 'Oh... and then you complain about me! You intrude on my relationship with Julie while you...'

'Your relationship with Julie is at the beginning; it can still be saved. Mine with Miranda has been going on for years. In fact, I should say it hasn't been going on for years.'

'It hasn't been going on because you are both stinking proud!' Well, now I notice I prefer to talk about him and Miranda. It takes my mind away from the idea of getting Julie back and maybe discovering that she has no intention of being "got back". 'Do you want advice? It doesn't matter, I'll give it to you anyway. This evening, come to the party that she's organising. If you don't settle things with her now, you risk losing each other forever.'

'And do you think that I... I can show up to her damn party like this?' He sits on the couch, pressing his palms to his forehead. 'Oh God, what a headache! It seems it's exploding! I must have got bronchitis... like a jerk! For that bitch...'

'I can call her and tell her you're going to die', I suggest with a good dose of cynicism. I can't help it; the effect is almost comical despite everything. I'm holding back so I won't laugh in his face. 'Maybe she'll take pity.'

'Yes, sure!' He opens his eyes angrily. I really try not to laugh, thinking about what Miranda's reaction might be. 'She doesn't even know what pity is! And anyway, I realised that you are taking advantage of my condition to distract me. So, hurry up and get Julie back while you can! Or she could really go back to her ex, believing you no longer care about her. Do you want to let that French asshole win?'

Julie

I don't know exactly what Valerie has in mind and above all why she asked me to meet in Grafton Street, in front of her favourite bag shop. Did she just feel like shopping today?

'Don't you have better things to do on Valentine's Day? Or are you looking for a gift for Stephen and need advice?' As soon as I see her emerge and approach me, I assail her with questions without even greeting her.

'Hi, my dear.' On the contrary, she takes the situation with exasperating calm and greets me by kissing both cheeks. 'Yes, that's it. I was thinking about something for Stephen. I hope I won't take up too much of your time. Oh, by the way... a few days ago I left my CV at the Irish souvenir shop, they called me for an interview, and there is a good chance they will hire me!'

She shows me the shop with a satisfied expression, then beckons me to walk along the road. I nod and follow her as she keeps talking and occasionally stopping as if to take time. She smiles often, and I realise I've never seen her so happy.

'Stephen took me to a really nice pub called The Stag's Head last night. On Friday and Saturday, they play live music. We must go all together!'

'Sure, we will go.'

I try to answer her and not dampen her enthusiasm with my bad mood. But I don't have much patience after meeting Philippe. And I don't even feel particularly inspired by the idea of looking for a Valentine's gift for a guy. On the contrary... I'm nervous, annoyed, tired. I just wish everything would pass quickly. Even the party and the dinner at Miranda's. This day, in short. I can't wait for everything to end and that it's already tomorrow!

We walk slowly, and I remain absorbed in my thoughts. Then I turn to Valerie. I don't know if she has already identified the appropriate shop and gift or is still looking for the right idea. She looks around and slows down almost to a stop, like she's looking for something or someone.

'Val... do you already have an idea of what you want to get for Stephen, or do you still have to think about it?'

She doesn't answer me and frowns. Then suddenly, she seems to light up; she nods and smiles. But not at me. She's pointing directly at the guy with the guitar down the street. I look at him, too; it's not my first time seeing him. With his long hair and a bit unkempt, he has his charm. I just don't understand why she doesn't move and we got stuck here.

When he starts the tune and the first words of a song, I stop entirely to listen to it. Valerie turns to me.

"Look into my eyes
You will see
What you mean to me
Search your heart
Search your soul
And when you find me there, you'll search no more
Don't tell me it's not worth tryin' for
You can't tell me it's not worth dyin' for
You know it's true
Everything I do
I do it for you..."

I recognise almost immediately *(Everything I do) I do it for you* by Bryan Adams. I breathe deeply and close my eyes for a moment. Then I open them again, ready to regain awareness of myself and follow Valerie in search of a gift for Stephen. But unexpectedly, I feel grabbed from behind, first by my arms and then by my waist. I turn around and find him in front of me.

'Maybe you'll still suffer from listening to another song, but this one...' he sighs and looks into my eyes. Then he bites his lips, and I realise he's embarrassed.

'Giles...' I rest my hands on his shoulders, and then I caress his cheeks. 'I... I'm sorry, I was stupid...'

'No, wait! About stupidity, yours and mine, we'll talk later.' He smiles and takes my hands. 'I don't want to waste the moment with this song in the background. Because that's the one where I... I tell you that I love you and I really... I'd do anything for you. I would have done it from the first moment.'

'Do you know what the truth is, Giles? That the other song, too, the one that made me think back to a bad moment... has not hurt me so much since I heard it again with you. The thought of you overwhelmed the previous pain because... I love you, too. And I was afraid; that's why I started to behave in a senseless way. I insisted you go out with Valerie...'

I look around to find my friend. She's a few steps away from us and smiling at me. Then she nods to Giles.

'You were...'

'Of course, we planned it!' Valerie comes close and strokes my back. 'We also asked the boy to sing this song specifically for you, and he was happy to help us. Miranda and I have hired him to play at the party tonight, so... it will be a great party!'

'Oh God, you're unbelievable!' I laugh and hide in Giles' arms.

'I wanted to sing it myself, but we agreed I was better not to.' Giles kisses my forehead and smiles, lifting my chin. 'You would have run away completely.'

'No, I wouldn't have run away.' I stroke his cheeks and kiss him on his lips. I feel observed by the world around us, passing people who slow down for a while, look at us and smile. But I don't care at this moment. I feel at peace with the world, in this city that is not mine, in this crowded street that has suddenly become familiar to me, friendly. 'I would have stayed until the end. Because I... I would do anything for you, too. You made me understand that nothing is worth it, not even my cooking course or my idea of becoming a food blogger when I really have no inclination for that job. Really, nothing is worth it; if trying to make it happen, I have to lose the person I love.'

CHAPTER 36

Miranda

Most likely, no one will show up. I learned from Valerie that the plan worked, and Juliette and Giles are back together. I'm happy for them; it's good that they found each other again. So, I will be alone with my single clients who have accepted the invitation and with my agency boys who don't have a "real" girlfriend to spend the evening with. And with the singer that Valerie convinced me to hire. I sincerely hope he has a repertoire that includes not only romantic songs because they would definitely be out of place.

Maybe by "no one", I mainly mean him. He has always been here, the previous years. Always. I don't even know why. Maybe as a perfect "St. Valentine's Secret Agent", he thought it appropriate to try to please me, his boss, and the available clients.

We have fixed the free premises on the same floor as the agency, as in previous years. I look around. It's still early, but it's all set. The main table and the decorations hanging on the windows and doors, the lights that follow each other. The environment seems warmer and more welcoming than usual this year. It almost seems like a party which doesn't exist on the official calendar but only here, in this corner of Finglas Village. A unique party in the world, halfway between Christmas and Valentine's Day. What I ordered has already arrived. I cooked some dessert, somehow. I'm not good at cooking, so I always prefer a catering company to prepare everything. The boys helped me with the decorations. Juliette had promised to bring something, but at this point... she'll probably be so busy with Giles that she won't even bring herself.

I snort and lean in front of the window that looks out on the street. Everything is dark and silent at this moment. Maybe I'm just a little envious of the others' happiness, that's it. Maybe...

I hear someone at the door; I jump and turn around. I pass the laid table and head to the entrance. I see Raymond enter, dressed in a dark blue elegant suit and a necktie around his neck. Literally clinging to his arm is Tally, who smiles at me not only with her lips but also with her sweet and innocent eyes. She's wearing a beautiful green wool dress and has a colourful cape on her shoulders. Multicoloured, as it has always been her style. She also wore a little make-up. I don't know who helped her, but they did an excellent job.

I greet them with a nod and a smile. I'm about to close because I don't expect to see Juliette and Giles appear behind them. Followed by Valerie and Stephen. Contrary to my assumptions, they are here. The boys are in elegant suits, like Raymond. Juliette and Valerie wear evening dresses under their coats and are wearing their make-up perfectly.

I massage my shoulders with both hands. If they thought they could surprise me, they succeeded. I remained in my jeans and a sweater that I wore to direct the catering and delivery operations of everything we needed for the party. Seen in this way, I look like a Cinderella who, instead of going to the ball, will sadly remain at home.

I realise my "famous" singles party is becoming a couples party, but it doesn't matter. I would rather leave them here and go away; I'm not in the mood. But I must carry on this farce, even if I'm in a bad mood. There are the clients to wait for, the other guys, the music to discuss with the singer...

In short, thinking about it, there is nothing that the others cannot do without me. So, I could leave everything and everyone and spin away to take refuge in my den with my favourite chocolates and maybe a movie. Not a romantic one, though.

'Thanks for being here, anyway. Although evidently...' I smile and shrug my shoulders. 'I think I'll go...' I must come up with a plausible excuse to disappear. I won't say that I have no intention of returning; I will put them in front of a fait accompli. 'I need to change, as you see. In the meantime, can you manage if someone comes, that would be all right? The singer is getting ready; maybe tell him to start playing something.'

I find myself stared at by six sceptical glances. Five, Tally is the only one to slightly tilt her face and look at me with an almost compassionate sweetness.

'Sure!' The first to answer is Giles. 'Well, we were actually thinking about organising events, so we can practice tonight. It would really be a great idea, what do you think?'

'Yes, I abandoned my stupid obstinacy to become a food blogger. I realised that I'm not that good. It's not for me. Instead, organising events and preparing parties like this would be great, that's it!' Juliette confirms the sensational idea of her boyfriend.

'We could talk about it. Tomorrow, maybe. I like the idea, too.' I say something just to please them and not give the impression of wanting to run away as quickly as possible.

'I'd like to think about the decorations, maybe the make-up.' Valerie also joins the chorus. I understand. Are we going to start a family business?

'I can think about the site! It will be fantastic; I already can imagine it.' Stephen's enthusiasm seems exaggerated to me. 'You know I also work as a website creator for some companies, don't you?'

'Yes, I know.' I cut it short because I don't want to link my thoughts to the one who won't come. 'All right, guys. We'll talk about it tomorrow, maybe.'

All I need now is for Raymond and Tally to offer themselves as entertainers. But why do I have a strange feeling that the one they're trying to entertain is actually me?

'I've already written several ideas down. I'm sure we'll have outstanding success!' Juliette smiles happily and hugs me. Then she bites her lips, trying to find something else to add. I think I know her by now. I know them all. They have something in mind in addition to the idea of organising events.

'Yes, of course...' I nod as I try to cross the human barrier they formed in front of me. I throw myself firmly towards the door. Maybe they're just trying to please me, and the idea isn't bad at all. But at this very moment, I feel suffocated; I can't stay a minute longer.

I pass a hand over my forehead; it almost feels like I have a temperature. And I feel like crying. Going through the door, I wipe my eyes; I can't stop myself anymore. I stay still for a moment, waiting for it to pass. Meanwhile, I hear the music coming from within; evidently, the guys have started to execute my orders to the letter.

I go downstairs and arrive on the ground floor; in my mind, I imagine myself already quiet at home, ready to vent all my tears. I lost him. I really lost him this time. And there is nothing that can bring him back to me. Nothing that can justify my behaviour, my terror of being hurt. Because in the end, I was really good at that. He didn't do me any harm; he tried to love me as he could, as he knew. It was me, with my own hands, who reached the goal of hurting myself.

'Miranda. Miranda Crossing... where do you think you're going?'

I'm not sure I can hear his voice just outside the lobby, past the glass door. Maybe it's just an illusion. Maybe one of the songs that comes from the room and reaches me here. A light but persistent rain is coming down. Of those that make using an umbrella useless because they get you wet anyway. I wipe my face with my hands repeatedly.

'Michael... you... What do you think you're doing out here?'

Michael

'I think I'll get the woman I love. I think I'll do everything I can to prevent her from escaping again.'

I don't know how firm and determined my voice is. I feel trembling from the cold and maybe also from the fever. When Giles almost forced me to show up here, I wasn't convinced at all. In fact, I was openly against it. But I couldn't stop myself. I failed trying to. I sent him a message telling him I would try to reach them. For the last time.

She sighs and continues to wipe her eyes. I'm not sure it's just rain. But it's still Miranda Crossing. Mine could only be a blunder due to fever.

'Hmm... good luck, then.'

In fact, she recovers quickly, straightens her shoulders, and gives me the usual hostile expression. Then, a hand furtively returns to touch her cheek. The other hand follows in rapid succession. No, it's not the rain.

'I'm afraid I'll have an extreme need of it.' I nod and step closer. But I feel myself staggering. I was lucky to be able to get here. I realise that everything they say about men and diseases is true. I'm a clear demonstration of it, knocked down by the flu! Destroyed, completely broken.

'Michael...' she sighs and shakes her head. Then she frowns and moves quickly towards me. She grabs me by the shoulders and then touches my forehead. 'Michael, but you... Oh God, you're burning!'

'Yes, well... at least I can always blame the fever if it goes wrong.'

'You didn't have to come up here in this condition!' She draws me close and puts her lips to my forehead.

'Apparently, it's not going that bad for me. It's better than the other times, at least. I was in the rain in front of your house last night.' I lower my face, and now her lips are within easy reach of mine. 'I knew you would send me away, but I didn't want to leave.'

'So you got sick, you got a fever...' She looks at me reproachfully, as if I was a disobedient child.

'I have had a fever since I met you. And I still haven't managed to let it pass.'

She closes her eyes and passes her arms around my neck. 'I believe... I have the same fever...'

'I love you, Miranda. I can't help it. Even if you're a bitch, most of the time. Even if you make my life like hell. I love you.'

'I know...' she sighs and strokes my arms; she breaks away from me to look into my eyes.

'What do you know? That you're a bitch or that I love you? In both cases, it's not great as an answer.'

She looks at me seriously, almost pouting. Then she opens into a radiant smile and holds me. Her face darkens again, and she looks back at me.

'Both things. I know I'm a bitch. And I know you love me. I love you too, Michael. This is why I tried to push you away in all the most subtle ways I could find. Because I was convinced that you could have a better life and be happier with someone else. Someone who wasn't marked by suffering as I am. A girl who could give you more than I can give you. Also, because you are so young, others might think...'

'I'd rather have what little you can grant me... than everything from another woman. I want you, Miranda. Today and for the next hundred Valentine's Days! I don't care about the rest of the world...'

She nods briefly and strokes my face. She gives me a sweet look for the first time since I've known her. An almost-in-love look.

'The truth is that love and happiness don't exist for some people unless shared with the rest of the world, exhibited in front of everyone. Everyone wants something or someone to show, Michael. Think of all the photos and posts published on social media. Everyone wants to show the world how beautiful, happy, and in love they are with their perfect smiles and relationships. I know it because it was the same for me before. But now I don't care about this kind of love anymore. I really want to love. I really want to be happy. Valentine's Day is just a day like any other. I want to be loved always. I want you.'

CHAPTER 37

Raymond

Why do people have so much difficulty understanding themselves and understanding each other? I can't explain it. I belong to a past generation where everything was perhaps more spontaneous and simpler. Not always, I realize. I loved, and I was loved by remarkable women. Maybe, unlike others, I learned to let go as I got older.

It's pointless to persist in suffering as Miranda did all this time. You only risk losing once again. Losing more, constantly losing. It's also pointless to let pride dominate, as Giles was doing with Juliette. Both proud and stubborn. Michael didn't give up; I must credit him for this. He fought for Miranda.

I have been here for many years, and I observe these lives that pass before me, touching my heart. In this ancient but modern city, in this corner of the world. In a cold winter that can only be warmed by love, by hope.

Miranda's pain has become my pain, day after day. I saw her grow, fight, and give up love until she tore her soul apart. I watched over her as I promised her Aunt Grace. I saw her carry on this business without caring at all about it. It was the only legacy she had received, after all. Try to give other women a bit of joy and romance. While she had eradicated this kind of feeling from her heart.

Pain and betrayal catch everyone unprepared. It caught Miranda in such a hard, devastating way. Not all people react in the same way. Miranda, unlike Valerie and Juliette, has built an armour around herself. Only patience and love have succeeded in breaking it down.

It's so true that love is always found in the most unexpected places. Sometimes, two hopeful eyes follow you gently, saying good morning and wishing you happiness. This happened to me with Tally.

I smile as the singer tunes in the Queen song *Crazy little thing called love*. Because love is truly a wonderful little craziness. We often don't realize it and forget to live it.

"This thing called love, I just can't handle it.
This thing called love, I must get round to it
I ain't ready
Crazy little thing called love."

We're all here now at the famous Miranda singles party. But there are no singles; there are no couples here. I see people happy to spend time together, sing, dance, and have fun. I see my Tally being moved as she receives affection and attention from people caring for her. Julie and Valerie did her make-up and dressed her in such an original and elegant way. Miranda and Michael, who, in the quiz organised for the party, are shamelessly cheating to let her win. Yes, that's just what I see. I only see love.

Tally

They say I won. I'm not sure, but I must trust them.

'I managed very well despite the fever. I'm a genius, in short.' Michael, the handsome green-eyed young man, laughs and surrounds Miranda with one arm.

'Oh, sure! My poor, misunderstood genius. Too bad we lost!' Miranda kisses him on his forehead, but he grabs her to kiss her lips. How beautiful Miranda is when she is happy! I have always told her that love would have reached her soon. That love was already with her. Finally, she decided to believe me.

'I'm sorry, I understood half of the questions. My English is not good enough!' The blonde girl, Valerie, laughs out loud. She lost, but she looks happy anyway.

'It doesn't matter; you'll make up for it later!' The handsome boy, Stephen, kisses her neck, and she laughs. I think I understood what he meant.

'I was distracted by the music...' Julie... or Juliette, as Miranda calls her, smiles and entices the other handsome boy, Giles, to dance with her. Her blue eyes shine with joy.

'I have corrupted the singer; I admit it!' Giles doesn't need to be asked twice and takes her in his arms.

The other people also smile. They say that I really won, all of them. A stay in a castle in England, I think. As a princess, they repeat to me, along with Raymond. He said he will also take me to Malahide Castle when we return to Dublin. And to visit all the castles of Ireland. This may make me feel even more like a princess, almost a queen.

I believe they are cheating me. I didn't win; it was them who kept making mistakes. I knew very little about the questions they asked in the game. Of some, I had a vague memory, lost in my past. In the days when my name was Stella, and I wasn't the poor tramp Tally. Yes, the poor tramp Tally, wishing everyone a future of love and happiness. The poor tramp Tally knew within herself that it would have come true for some.

So, they helped me guess, especially Miranda and Michael. And now everyone says I won. They have a good heart. They really make me feel like a princess, worthy of a castle. Maybe they understood that I wanted to live a fairy tale. Maybe they read between my desires, my hopes, my dreams. The fairy tale that, in all my life, I never had, I never managed to achieve. Yes, that's exactly what they gave me.

'It will be like a fairy tale.' I say it out loud, almost surprising myself.

'Yes, Tally. It will be like a fairy tale.' Miranda nods, approaches me, and surrounds my shoulders with one arm. 'Because every woman in every situation she finds herself is entitled to a fairy tale. Thanks for helping me believe it.'

I kiss her cheek. Raymond approaches and takes my hand.

'May I have this dance, princess?'

I smile and follow him. They really gave me a fairy tale, these people. And now I have a prince as well. I look at them and perceive their dreams, their projects. I can read between their thoughts.

Juliette and Giles want to discover the wonders of Ireland and then go to Paris. He plans to do something for her on a tower called Eiffel or something like that. Valerie and Stephen will visit Australia. Miranda and Michael... will have a story to tell, a long story with a happy ending.

There will be a castle for me and my Raymond. It may be my own castle. I'm a princess, after all. Because Miranda, for once, was right.

Every woman, in any situation she finds herself in, is entitled to a fairy tale. She just has to find the courage to believe it

PLAYLIST

Elton John: "Something about the way you look tonight"

George Michael: "One more try"

Bryan Adams: "(Everything I do) I do it for you"

Queen: "Crazy little thing called love"

ACKNOWLEDGEMENTS

I always find myself in trouble when I get to the end of a story. I feel forced to abandon the characters who have accompanied me for part of my journey. This time is no different.

On Valentine's Day, I wanted and tried to tell a story different from the others, which revolves around multiple points of view. Four, particularly those of Julie, Giles, Miranda, and Michael. Above all, my purpose was to write an interlinked story in which the events and destinies of the characters follow each other, fit together, and intertwine more and more. One fact follows the other, and everyone meets on the streets of Dublin to live, dream, and love.

Dublin, for the first time a setting of one of my stories, was an exciting and complex challenge at the same time. I've learned to know it simultaneously with the writing of the novel and almost simultaneously with the protagonists.

I wanted to portray love stories between characters different in temper, age, origin, and experiences. I tried to show a sort of uprooting from one's roots which, however, in a certain sense, unites everyone in a new home, in a new dimension, that from being a stranger becomes increasingly familiar, welcomed, enlivened by Dublin and Ireland. Thus, as the reference points become more solid and tangible, the relationships of friendship and love between the characters are also strengthened and intensified.

I thank, as always, those of you who wanted to read my story and be part of this new adventure. Your support is invaluable to me. I thank the music that, as always, accompanies my stories by giving melody and rhythm to my characters' experiences and events.

I thank Dublin and Ireland for their charm on me, allowing me to carry out this project. I thank the places I have mentioned and on which my gaze has repeatedly settled recently. With all my heart, I thank Joseph, who helped me discover them by walking me through the streets of Dublin. This book exists because of you, only because of you.

Thanks to Ghostly Whisper Ltd. and my proofreaders, who are so precious to me.

I thank my family for always supporting me since I started writing, all my life basically.

I hope you spent a few delightful hours with my characters and that their stories and love have helped you dream a little. Because (as Tally said at the end) I believe every reader as well, in any situation, is entitled to a fairy tale. Thanks to you, in this case, for helping me believe in it.

About the author:

Facebook: https://www.facebook.com/BarbaraMorganAuthor

Instagram: https://www.instagram.com/barbaramorganbooks/

Twitter: https://twitter.com/BabsiMorgan

www.ingramcontent.com/pod-product-compliance
Lightning Source LLC
Chambersburg PA
CBHW020413180626
46812CB00003B/961